MajikQuest
The Urith Adventure

Trace Richards

Twisted River Press, LLC
Fantasy

Louisiana, Missouri

This is a work of fiction. All the characters and events portrayed in this book are either products of the author's imagination or are used fictitiously.

MajikQuest: The Urith Adventures
Copyright © 2013 Trace Richards

Cover art and illustrations by Crash Daniels
Copyright © 2013

First Published by Twisted River Press, LLC.
Twisted River Press
815 Tennessee
Louisiana, MO 63353
www.twistedriverpress.com

ISBN: 978-0-9828218-4-8
First Edition: May 2013

Printed in the United States of America

For Theresa Hoffman and all of the RPG gamers out there.

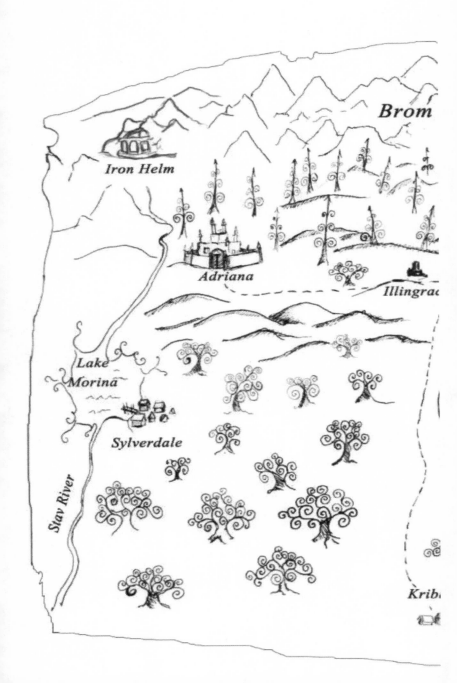

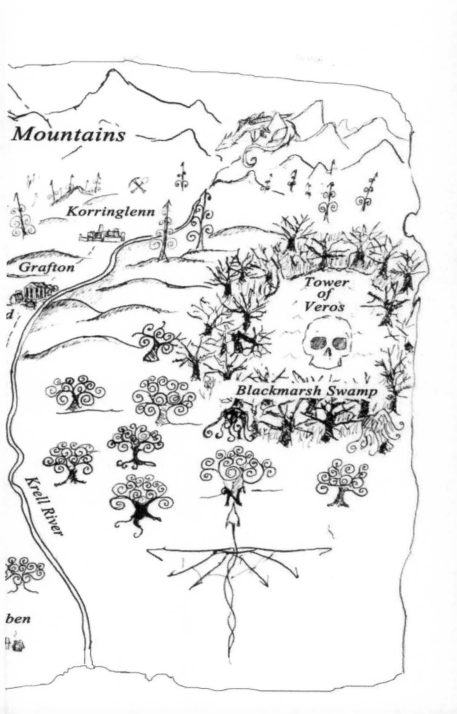

MajikQuest
The Urith Adventure

PROLOGUE

The Gathering of Heroes

The fiery sun blazed brightly over the distant hills. Tree limbs swayed in a gentle breeze, the rustling sounds of the leaves easily heard throughout the otherwise quiet neighborhood. Beneath a bright blue sky, four bicycles sped along the street, three of which were ridden by teenaged boys while a girl of a similar age manned the last. Clad in casual t-shirts, jeans, and sneakers, they raced on. Each carried a backpack and gazed ahead with determined eyes. Faster they peddled, as though the fate of the world rested upon their young shoulders.

Veering from the street, the group rode their bikes into the front yard of a single-story, red-brick house with a garage attached to its side. Dropping their bikes to rest in the lush grass, they marched to the front door, the boy in the lead quickly ringing the doorbell. A few moments passed before the door opened to reveal a short-haired, middle-aged woman.

Garbed in a red V-neck shirt and a long white skirt, she smiled at the youths. The smell of baked confectioneries emanated from within the dwelling behind her.

"Hello, Mrs. Mckanahan," the youth said.

"Hi, Jake... Peter... Josh... Amy..." Mrs. Mckanahan said in reply, acknowledging the others that were present as well. "Kevin is waiting downstairs. C'mon in..."

Stepping inside, each of the four kicked their shoes off to leave them near the doorway before making their way across the kitchen's white tile. Opening a door at the opposite side of the room, they descended a series of wooden steps in single file.

Cool concrete caressed the soles of their feet through the white cotton of their socks at the bottom of the steps. Walls of gray brickwork surrounded them as they made their way past a black washer and dryer to a large red throw rug near the basement's center. A sturdy wooden coffee table sat over the rug with a couch oriented to accommodate its length on each side, a two-seater on the left and a three-seater on the right. A large recliner of tan leather sat at one end, the impression that it was to be the table's head implied by its position.

On the wall behind the recliner was a large, colorful world map that seemingly displayed, not this world, but another. Elaborately hand drawn with colored markers, it resembled a great archipelago with clustered islands of various sizes surrounding three larger land masses. Each of the many islands were labeled with names. The large words at the top proclaimed that the map showed the World of Urith.

Paper, pencils, and a large pink eraser covered the surface of the coffee table, along with several smaller gridded maps. There was an assortment of small figurines, many of which seemed to be made in the likeness of medieval beings such as knights or wizards and strange mythological creatures such as goblins, ogres, trolls, or dragons. An assortment of odd dice was scattered about, as well. While some had the typical six sides, others seemed to be capable of different results. One that resembled a pyramid seemed to only be able to generate numbers from one to four, while other multifaceted shapes had digits ranging from one to eight, ten, twelve, or even twenty.

A rectangular sheet of cardboard, folded into three equal sections was erected at the table's head. The front of the screen bore pictures of yet more medieval characters and fantastic beasts, and the words *MajikQuest* stretched across its top in letters of vibrant gold. A stack of three books titled *Player's Tome, Majik Master's Tome,* and *Tome of Monsters,* respectively, sat before the screen, as well.

Seated at the table's head, a teenaged boy with dark brown hair and glasses looked up from behind the screen. The black t-shirt that he wore sported the fearsome visage of a green dragon on its front. "Hey, guys," he said.

"What's up, Kevin?" Josh replied.

Sitting on the couch to Kevin's left was a younger girl clad in a simple bright red t-shirt and blue jeans; one known by all that was present to be his sister Jennifer, who was younger than him by two years. Long strands of thick brown hair hung over her shoulders, and her hands rested in her lap. Her back rested against one of the couch's arm rests for support as her crossed legs extended the length of the seat, her toes occasionally wiggling within a pair of red socks.

"Is she playing?" Peter asked as Jennifer turned to rest her feet on the floor.

"Afraid so," Kevin sighed. "Her friend who she usually hangs out with is away with her parents to visit family out of state, and she wanted to play. Mom said we have to let her, and she's baking cookies for us, so I'm not gonna argue with her."

Amy smirked. Jennifer had watched them play the game several times before. Usually asking a lot of questions during the game, she tended to get on Kevin's nerves with constant interruptions and had never actually been allowed by her older brother to participate until now. "Finally...another girl in the group," she said, delighted that the game now had a slightly stronger matriarchal presence.

"It's fine with me," Jake chimed in as he, Josh, and Peter all sat their packs aside, taking a seat upon the longer couch while Amy claimed the place next to Jennifer as her own. "Now I got someone else to pick on besides Amy."

"If I remember right, Jake, the last time you picked on me, it cost you a few gold pieces," Amy retorted with a playful grin.

Kevin handed everyone a sheet of paper labeled *MajikQuest Character Record Sheet* across the top. "You planning on playing a thief again, Amy?"

"I dunno yet," she replied. "Maybe I'll play a warrior this time and just kick the dwarf's ass when he gets mouthy instead of pilfering his coin pouch."

"And how do you know I'm gonna play a dwarf again?" Jake asked.

"Because you always play a dwarf," Peter answered before Amy had a chance. "You always play a dwarf who likes to smack the ass of every barmaid we see and who spends most of his gold on booze."

"Kinda like his shirt says," Josh added, pointing to the black t-shirt the plump youth wore, the front of which bared a comical depiction of a dwarf who held up a foamy mug, the text over him proclaiming in bold white letters, *I spent my gold on ale and whores.*

"Hey, I've played a human a few times," Jake protested.

Kevin grinned.

"Yes, you have, and they usually spend their gold on ale and whores, too."

Jennifer began looking over the sheet in her possession. "What are Might, Agility, Stamina, Intellect, Wisdom, and Charisma?" she asked while scanning over a list which represented the main attributes of a character in the game.

"Here, lemme help you out," Amy volunteered as she had seated herself next to the younger girl. "Us girls are gonna have to stick together here."

Pulling out their own copies of the *Player's Tome* and spiral notebooks from their backpacks, all at the table soon began rolling dice to generate the statistics that would represent the fictional personae they would be portraying in the game.

Each knew the rules of the roleplaying game well enough. It worked through a combination of storytelling, improvised voice acting, and dice rolling. Kevin would serve as the game's Majik Master, a role that was one part storyteller and one part game referee. Through this role, he would weave an intricate story plot and set up challenges for the others to guide their characters through as they worked toward whatever would be the ultimate goal of that particular game.

While watching over the rest of his friends, Kevin Mckanahan thought back on the years that he and the others had played the game. He first discovered it in the middle of his eighth grade year while attending a yard sale with his mother one Saturday. He had always had a fondness for medieval fantasy, and with a little bit of convincing, his mother bought the game for him. He had been fortunate that the three hardback books and dice were being sold as a set, because later he discovered that each had to be purchased separately through book and hobby stores.

For the remainder of that weekend, he had perused over the three rulebooks that the game was comprised of, learning how to generate the characters and run adventures as the game's host. Returning to school the following Monday, he quickly told his closest friends, Jake Steinman, Josh Traynor, and Peter Wellington, about *MajikQuest*. The four had quickly planned a sleepover at Kevin's house that weekend to play.

The boys were immediately hooked, spending their entire weekend in Kevin's basement while guiding their characters throughout a fantastic world of his design. The remainder of the year passed as their game continued, their adventures culminating with a quest to save the king when a malevolent prince sought to usurp his throne.

Amy Linderman joined the boys soon after the start of their freshman year in high school, as she happened to spot Kevin and the others one day with the game books at a table during lunch. As a new student at the school who had just gone through her first week, Amy had yet to make many friends. She and her two best friends had actually played the game together before she and her parents had moved there so that her father could pursue a career offer he had gotten.

Amy wasted no time approaching the boys about the game and soon joined them to play on a regular basis. The adventures in the basement of the Mckanahan home took place nearly every weekend and even through one entire summer. Sometimes, Kevin would run short adventures with characters that would only be played once, since at times one or more members of their social circle would be unable to join for one reason or another. Their near obsession with the game had lasted all the way to their current sophomore years in high school.

Kevin's thoughts returned to the present as he finished some last-minute preparations for the adventure, his rolls and notes hidden from the eyes of the other players behind his screen. Within the span of an hour, the others at the table had finished designing their characters.

Everyone handed their finished characters to Kevin to look over. "Looks like a fairly well balanced party," he commented while flipping through the sheets. "A good mix of magic and combat ability."

"Peter's character and mine are gonna be childhood friends again," Jake stated.

"Fair enough," Kevin replied. "Do you have a backstory for your character, Amy?"

"I haven't put much thought into it," Amy admitted. "She probably learned her swordsmanship from someone in her family—her father, maybe."

"I wouldn't know where to start coming up with a backstory for my character," Jennifer said.

"It's ok," Josh said. "I don't have anything really thought up, either. I figure he's just always been with the church and hasn't seen a whole lot of excitement up 'til this point."

"Hey, whatever's clever," Kevin said. "I'll have to figure out how I'm gonna work my sister into the game, but it'll come to

me. I'll come up with a history on the fly for her, as well."
Jennifer grinned as Kevin handed the character sheets back to
the players. "Let's get the adventure started."

CHAPTER
1
The Quest Begins

The songs of birds could be heard all across the peaceful countryside. Grassy hills rose in the distance beneath a clear blue sky. The trees of a forest dotted the area behind a tall and slender young woman who cast her gaze down from atop a steep hill.

Standing in the center of a dirt road, the woman's left hand rested upon the golden hilt of a long sword, the blade of which was sheathed in a scabbard that hung at her side from a reddish leather belt. With a casual sweep of her right hand, she brushed a few strands of her lengthy blonde hair from her eyes as a warm summer breeze sent it trailing through the air. Garbed in a tan vest, brown leggings, and soft tan boots with fur tops, she stared at her intended destination with glassy blue eyes.

A backpack of tanned leather and a small round shield of sturdy metal hung from her back, the front of which bore the depiction of a rearing horse with long feathery wings—a legendary creature known as a Pegasus. She grinned while adjusting a pair of fur-trimmed leather bracers that were around her wrists.

Not much further, Alaina...

With a confident stride, the woman made her way on down the path, her steps taking her toward a small town that lay in the distant valley below.

Growing up an only child on a patch of farmland near a small town known as Kribben, Alaina Swiftblade had always yearned for adventure. She enjoyed the many tales that she had heard the bards tell, stories of bold adventurers who delved into dangerous dungeons and bravely faced fearsome creatures. Not wanting to be a victim of the world's monsters or villains, she sought to learn all she could of swordsmanship from her father, a soldier who had fought in two wars before a third finally took his life. Illness claimed her mother two years later, leaving her alone at the age of nineteen.

With a small amount of gold and silver coins that had been left to her by her parents, she bought some of the essential equipment and gear that most adventurers needed in their travels, items such as a tent and bedroll, flint and steel for starting fires, dry food rations, a wineskin for water, and a hooded oil lantern. Armed with the sword of her father, she acquired a shield from a local armorer and left her old life behind. A month's time had since passed, and now she wandered the lands, using the warrior skills she had learned from her father in her search of adventure and fortune.

Alaina looked around as she entered the small town. She would have to ask one of the locals that moved about in their daily endeavors for information on the area, as she had never learned to read and could glean nothing of her whereabouts from the wooden sign that greeted her upon arrival. Well-constructed and maintained buildings of wood and stone stood on both sides of the dirt road as she walked on. A wagon full of wooden barrels approached, drawn by four large draft horses. A bald, yet heavily bearded, and solidly built man held the reins. Garbed in a loose-fitting white shirt, brown trousers, and hard boots of black leather, he gave a friendly nod of his head as his eyes met hers. "Hail," Alaina called out, aiming an upraised open palm to him.

Pulling the reigns, the teamster brought the wagon to a halt beside her. "Well met, traveler," he replied while looking down, his voice thick with rolling consonants.

Alaina gave a friendly smile. "Could you tell me in what town I have arrived and direct me to food and lodgings?"

The teamster stroked his thick, dark beard. "Aye, I could," he started. "This be Grafton. You'll find the Golden Tankard that-a-way." He turned and pointed down the road behind him. "About eight buildings down and to yer left. Ya can't miss it, lass."

"Much obliged," Alaina said.

"Safe journeys to you, traveler," the teamster replied before ushering the horses on again. The wagon's round wooden wheels churned up bits of dust as Alaina paused briefly to watch it depart before continuing down the road, mindful of the buildings to her left.

Eight structures down, Alaina came to a two-story building of off-white brick. The sounds of rowdy laughter spilled out from beyond the establishment's open doorway. Above the entrance, a whitewashed wooden sign hung from an outstretched pole.

While Alaina again found the sign's writing to be incomprehensible, she surmised that she had found the inn by the image of a large mug overflowing with a frothy brew that was painted on it. Alaina grinned.

Looks like this is the place...

Stepping through the doorway, she peered inside. Firelight flickered about the tavern's interior from lit sconces on the walls. Round tables and chairs sat everywhere about the wooden floor. A trio of serving wenches moved about the masses, an occasional whistle or cat call directed at them as they saw to the needs of the patrons that were seated at every turn.

Many of the people were engaged in card or dice games as they partook of the food and drink. The bar at the back of the establishment was equally crowded. A stout-looking bartender hastily filled mugs with ale from the kegs along the wall as thirsty men seated along the bar's length gulped down the potent brew.

Alaina scanned the scene for several seconds in search of a vacant spot to sit. To her left, she finally spotted an empty booth among several others that were occupied. Making her way through the sea of rowdy, beer-swilling people, she set her pack and shield down beside her and claimed the seat.

A barmaid soon approached. The folds of the plump woman's green dress flowed with her movement. Over a loose-fitting white shirt, a tan corset was laced up to lift her bosom to a position that men would find more pleasing to look at. "Welcome to the Golden Tankard," she said, smiling down at Alaina. "How may I serve you?"

The sounds of clashing steel and cries of battle rang throughout the forest. A bellow of pure rage erupted from deep within a red-bearded dwarf to resonate off of the trunks of the trees. Armored in a suit of scale mail with a horned metal helmet atop his head, he charged his foes with a round steel shield in his left hand and an upraised battle ax in his right. His black eyes shone with a determined fury, his course undaunted as several arrows sailed past his short, stocky form.

The targets of his ire were but fifteen feet away—tall, burly, humanoid creatures with a brownish, hairy hide. Armored in hardened leathers with crude animal hides and furs, their visages were apelike with large pointed ears. Reddish eyes glared menacingly from beneath metal helmets as they readied their bows to launch more arrows.

Two more arrows flew past the dwarf, shots that were suddenly fired from behind him to drop two of his enemies with fatal hits in the stomach. He crashed into the third, embedding his axe into the creature's chest with a sick, wet sound before it could fire another shot. Bracing a black leather boot against the humanoid's chest, the dwarf dislodged his bloody weapon with an upward yank before turning to the one who had aided him. "Hey, Darrius," he yelled gruffly. "You know what I hate about hobgoblins?"

A few yards away was the slender form of an elf. Clad in a green tunic, tan leggings, and soft brown boots, he dashed forward. A bow was grasped in his left hand as he drew another arrow, the fletching of many more visible as they peeked over his right shoulder from a quiver on his back. His long blonde hair whipped in the air as he ducked an axe blade that came for his head.

Moving with a liquid grace, he slew the attacking hobgoblin as he plunged the still-grasped arrow into its abdomen. Jerking the arrow out moments before the hobgoblin fell, he stood once more to swiftly knock and draw it.

"What's that, Grimm?" he asked, answering the dwarf's question with one of his own as he loosed the arrow to fell another enemy.

Grimm raised his shield in time to intercept the descent of a heavy mace. The impact of the weapon forced a grunt out of him. "The damn smell," he answered through clenched teeth as he swung the axe around to slay another of the humanoids.

Grimm Ironforge and Darrius Goldleaf had been close friends for many a year. Their fathers had become equally inseparable in the course of their many adventures as they stood side by side battling orcs, goblins, trolls, and many other creatures. Grimm and Darrius were now at the ages of forty and ninety, respectively, and fate seemed to have similar plans for them, as well.

The forest grew silent once more as the remnants of the hobgoblins fell, two more struck by arrows from Darrius' bow while a third and fourth were cut down by Grimm's axe. The bodies of many foes lay about the ground as the elf and dwarf both turned to the distant valley. Many more of the warmongering creatures could be seen below as they descended on a distant town.

Darrius frowned.

"They're going to raid Grafton! That town barely has five hundred people. They'll never survive the onslaught!"

Taking off in a full sprint down the hill, he glanced back at Grimm. "C'mon... we have to hurry!"

Grimm ran to follow, his short, stocky legs proving to have difficulty in keeping up with the longer stride of his taller, pointy-eared companion. "Hey!" he called out. "Wait for me!"

A white, curved ceiling rose high overhead. Beams of sunlight poured in through stained glass windows that bore colorful patterns of red, green, blue, and gold. Two rows of sturdy wooden pews formed a long aisle amid white walls as a vibrant red carpet stretched along its length to end at a white stone altar. A red tapestry with gold trim covered its surface along with many long, slender white candles. The flames of the candles danced and flickered above a hefty mace that lay beneath them.

Before the altar knelt a young man. Brown, lamb's-wool-like hair covered his head, and his form was cloaked in robes of white and gold. His hands were clasped before his chest as his gentle green eyes gazed upward. On the wall high above was a huge golden idol that was in the likeness of a blazing sun. Closing his eyes, he lowered his head in silence.

"Powers of Light, hear my prayers..."

Even as a young boy, Halvar Lightbringer had always wanted to help people, and it was this desire that brought him to join the clergy at the age of just fifteen. Throughout his apprenticeship, he read the teachings of the order through ancient scrolls; how the Powers had created the world of Urith and all life therein.

In an eternal struggle, the Powers of Light stood against the Powers of Darkness in their attempts to corrupt and control the world, and it was the priests' role to ensure that such corruption was opposed at every turn. Halvar was somewhat familiar with the beliefs of the other orders as well and could even agree with some of their teachings. The Powers of Law likewise struggled against the Powers of Chaos in a similar manner, and the Powers of Balance mediated to ensure that none gained too much in their cosmic struggles. Now at twenty years of age, Halvar believed that he had found his place in the grand design as a cleric of the Powers of Light.

Through faith in The Powers and their cosmic plans, the clerics of the various orders were capable of performing miraculous feats. With the might of their deities channeled through them, they could smite down enemies, drive away evil spirits, or heal the sick and injured. Some rare individuals even had faith strong enough to return the recently deceased to life.

As Halvar knelt in silence, sounds from outside caught his ear. Opening his eyes, he listened for a moment as he tried to discern what it was he had heard, the distant roar becoming louder as he soon realized that he was hearing the screams of a panicked crowd. Quickly claiming his mace from atop the altar, Halvar rushed up the aisle toward the temple doors.

This can't be happening...

In wide-eyed terror, a young woman in a loose-fitting white shirt and light blue leggings watched as the apelike humanoids ransacked the town, carnage ensuing in the course of their sudden raid. Divana Nadrey remembered witnessing such horror before, as her hometown of Illingrad had at one time been raided by hobgoblins; their attacks on human settlements well-known and feared. Her mother, father, and older sister were cut down by the beasts, as she and several others among the townsfolk had been taken prisoner to be used as slaves when she was but twelve years of age.

Had it not been for the arrival of a powerful wizard who came to rescue her and the others, her future would surely have been short. Taken in by the high wizard soon after this, she became one of two apprentices to him and had been practicing the arcane arts under his guidance ever since.

All around, the panic-stricken men and women fled for their lives. Some were grabbed by the hobgoblins, kicking and screaming as they were dragged away, while others were cut down without mercy by the axes and swords of the humanoids.

Divana gasped in fright as one of the hobgoblins suddenly locked its bloodshot eyes on her. With its axe grasped firmly in both hands, it started to advance. Slowly, the creature began to raise its weapon. Divana fearfully backed away, her green eyes wide with fright. She wished that Jerrod, her peer as apprentice to Agamemnon, were here to help her face the vile humanoid. With a roar, the hobgoblin suddenly charged.

Divana flung her right arm out, her middle and index fingers extended to point at her aggressor.

"Arrak Alabarr!" she cried out in a bold tone.

The folds of her loose fitting white shirt whipped about her arms. Strands of her long red hair trailed through the air as a crackling bolt of arcane energy flew from her fingertips. The hobgoblin's eyes widened in surprise just moments before the bolt struck it in the chest.

Divana cautiously approached the fallen creature. With the toe of a brown leather boot, she nudged its side. Catching sight of a searing wound in its chest, she sighed as relief flooded her. The creature had been slain.

Mastery of magic was mentally testing, and thus far she could only commit one spell at a time to memory. Mystic Bolt was one that she had hoped she would never have to use, yet it was one that she always memorized in case she should ever need to defend herself. On this day, it had saved her life.

If only I were as powerful a mage as Agamemnon…

The high wizard was the only hope that Divana knew of to save Grafton from this threat. Whirling about amid the panic, she pondered running back to Illingrad. She knew the high wizard could be found in his tower there. Illingrad was two miles to the west, however. She knew that by the time she reached Agamemnon, it would be too late to save the town.

Suddenly, she heard a high-pitched scream split the air, a cry that seemed to be born of rage rather than fright. Stopping to turn around, she spotted a woman charging out of the Golden Tankard Inn across the street.

Garbed in fur-trimmed tans and browns, the woman was clearly a warrior, as she brandished a shield and sword. Long blonde hair whipped through the air with her movements as she lifted her shield to successfully block an in-coming axe before bringing her sword around with an overhead slash to slay the attacking hobgoblin. A back hand swing with the sword cut down a second one before it could bring down an upraised club.

"Filthy hobgoblins." Alaina spat.

Two more of the vile humanoids rushed in, one wielding a spear while the second swung a flail over its head. Twirling around, Alaina parried a spear jab with her sword before bashing the hobgoblin with her shield. The hobgoblin crashed to the ground as Alaina quickly brought her sword down to finish it off.

Turning to face the second, Alaina barely managed to duck the spiked ball of a flail that snaked out along a length of chain before retaliating with an upward backhand slash of her sword. The blade cut across the hard leather chest plate that covered the hobgoblin, knocking it backward. Although the blade had cut it badly, the armor had protected it enough to stop the blow from being a killing one. Alaina lunged quickly, driving her sword into the creature's belly and out again before it could regain its balance. A sick gurgling sound crept out of the hobgoblin as it crumpled to the ground in a fetal position.

As Divana watched the battle, she suddenly spotted a hobgoblin down the street. With a look of malice, the creature aimed a bow at the warrior woman.

"Look out!" Divana warned as the arrow was loosed.

A sharp pain shot through Alaina's right leg as the arrow found its mark. Clenching her teeth, she fell to the ground; her sword dropping from her grasp as she reflexively grabbed the shaft of the arrow in her leg. The hobgoblin drew a second arrow.

Struggling through the pain in her leg, Alaina raised her shield. She winced as a second arrow tanked off of its metal surface, followed seconds after by a third. Peeking over the top of her shield to check her attacker's position, she spotted the hobgoblin as it reached over its shoulder to draw another arrow from a quiver on its back. Suddenly, the creature let out a loud shriek as it sprawled face first to the ground.

A tall and slender man stood over the creature, his form cloaked in robes of white and gold as he held a sturdy mace in his hand. Wasting no time, he ran toward Alaina, quickly kneeling beside her.

"You're hurt..." Halvar observed.

Alaina screamed as she quickly yanked the arrow from her leg, casting it aside as Divana joined them. "More of them are coming!" she said, looking down the road toward more hobgoblins that were rushing in.

Alaina fell onto her back, exhausted from her struggle. Halvar frowned as he examined her wound.

"Let me help you," he said.

Placing his hands over the injury, he lifted his head and closed his eyes.

"Powers of Light, mend this brave warrior's broken body so that she may yet serve the cause of good."

Alaina and Divana watched as Halvar's hands began to glow with a soft light. Alaina suddenly felt the pain in her leg subside. "Wow!" Divana exclaimed as Alaina reclaimed her sword and struggled to her feet. Readying her weapon and shield again, she glared at the charging hobgoblins.

"You won't take this town without a fight," she growled.

Halvar stepped up to her side. "Stay behind us," he instructed Divana. "We will protect you as best we can."

Alaina and Halvar readied themselves to receive the charging hobgoblins as Divana backed away. An arrow suddenly struck one of the hobgoblins in the side of the neck. Another one soon followed to strike in a similar fashion, halting the hobgoblins' advance as all turned to see who had now joined the battle. Standing with a bow drawn was an elf. He launched another arrow at the hobgoblins as a stout-looking dwarf charged past him, a bloody axe in hand.

"An elf and a dwarf," Alaina observed while she and Halvar dashed forward.

"It seems that the Powers have brought us together," Halvar said.

More arrows flew from the elf's bow as he slowly began to advance. "Don't let them divide us, Grimm!" he warned the dwarf, who crashed into one of the hobgoblins with his shield. Grimm turned briefly to his companion after bringing his axe down on the prone hobgoblin. "Behind you, Darrius!"

Spinning quickly, Darrius spotted a hobgoblin rushing toward him, an upraised mace held high over its head. Sidestepping the attack, he drew a large Kukri knife from his side with an underhand grip. Lashing out, he cut the humanoid's throat with one deft slash of the inward curving blade before turning to face the others. Flipping his grip on the knife to an overhand one, he threw it to stick into the heart of another of the hobgoblins as it smashed a sword into Alaina's raised shield.

Nodding her head to Darrius in gratitude, Alaina spun around to slay another foe with a horizontal slash across its abdomen as Grimm hacked and slashed wildly to bring two more of them down.

"There's too many of 'em," Alaina panted as she turned to spot Halvar, who had squared off with another of the creatures.

Halvar swung his mace as the hobgoblin blocked the attack with its shield. The creature seemed to sneer at him as it prepared to attack.

"Now you die, human," it growled.

Halvar raised his mace, pointing it to the heavens.

"Powers of Light, lend me thy might so that I may vanquish this servant of evil!"

The mace suddenly began to glow in Halvar's hand as though it were wreathed in white flames. His white robes furled as he charged. A look of surprise in the hobgoblin's eyes as it again raised its shield. Halvar's mace struck the hobgoblin's protection once more, this time shattering the sturdy wooden shield. The creature shrieked in pain as the force of the blow launched it across the street. It crashed through the side of a parked cart, the straw that filled it burying the creature as it flowed out through the ruptured side.

With a furrowed brow, Halvar turned to Alaina. "You got one hell of a swing." She smirked.

Meanwhile, Divana watched the battle from several yards away. A brilliant flash of light at her back suddenly caught her attention. Turning, she spotted an elderly man in flowing green robes. Long white hair framed his wrinkled visage from beneath a tall, pointed hat that matched his attire in color. A white beard flowed past a length of simple rope that was tied around his waist. In his hands, a long, gnarled staff was erected as he gazed at the battle with an intense stare.

"Agamemnon!" Divana cried out.

The high wizard flung out his left arm while aiming the staff with his right. His robes and hair began to flow as though caught in a wind. "Mirroth! Arrak Alabarr!" he called out with a commanding voice.

The end of the staff glowed and crackled with power. Several Mystic Bolts flew from the staff toward the combatants, darting around the heroes to strike, as only the hobgoblins were the targets of the wizard's wrath. Screeches and howls of fright soon followed the display of power as the hobgoblins quickly began to fall back. "Retreat!" one of them growled. "Retreat!"

Alaina and Halvar watched as the creatures fled from Grafton. A volley of arrows from Darrius' bow ensured that their flight continued as Grimm's axe ended the life of one more that yet remained. All was soon silent, as the battle had reached its conclusion. The townspeople cautiously began to venture out from the homes and places of business in which they had locked themselves.

"Is everyone alright?" Halvar asked as all who had participated in the battle had joined him.

"I think so," Alaina answered. "Thank you for healing my leg. Are you a cleric of the temple here?"

Halvar nodded. "Indeed. I am Halvar Lightbringer, servant of the good."

"Alaina Swiftblade," she replied with a grin before turning to the elf and dwarf who had aided them.

"I am Darrius Goldleaf," the elf said before gesturing to the dwarf. "This is my friend, Grimm Ironforge." Grimm only grunted while giving a nod of his head.

"My name is Divana Nadrey," Divana said before turning to the elderly wizard that towered over her. "This is..."

"High wizard Agamemnon," Grimm interrupted gruffly. "It's an honor to meet you."

"Please excuse my companion," Darrius interjected. "He can be a bit rude at times. We have heard much about you, as both of our fathers journeyed with you for many a year. It is a pleasure to meet you as well young Divana. Are you an apprentice of the high wizard?"

Divana smiled. "Yes, I am."

We are grateful for your aid," Halvar said.

As the conversation continued, Alaina suddenly noticed the approach of a slender, dark-haired man. Appearing to be perhaps in his early fifties, he was immaculately groomed, with hints of gray only just beginning to show in the sides of his hair. He was clad in a fine red tunic and brown breeches. His boots of black leather kicked up dust from the road as he rushed toward the group with worry and fear etched in his face.

All turned to face him as he stopped before Agamemnon.

"High Wizard, I am Derrik Grunswald, mayor of Grafton, and I am in dire need of your services."

"An introduction is not required, Mayor Grunswald," Agamemnon said. "What is your need?"

Mayor Grunswald tried desperately to compose himself before continuing.

"My daughter Alyssa... she's been taken by those things, along with several others. I'll gladly pay you for her safe return. She's but fifteen. Please help me!"

The high wizard smiled. "I assure you that your daughter will be returned to you safely," he said reassuringly. "This is not a quest for me, however."

He turned to Alaina, Halvar, Grimm, and Darrius.

"This... is a quest for you, brave heroes."

"Two hundred gold pieces will be yours to divide amongst yourselves if you can bring her back safely," Mayor Grunswald offered.

Halvar nodded. "By the Powers of Light, your daughter will be returned to you," he proclaimed.

"And you will accompany them," Agamemnon added, placing an acknowledging hand on Divana's shoulder. "This world is full of dangers, but experience in it will do you much good. You will make the necessary preparations for this journey, and you will then accompany these brave heroes." With uncertainty in her eyes, Divana nodded.

"I, too, have preparations to make," Halvar added. "I must return to the temple and gather a few things. We'll meet back at the inn before departing."

"Fair enough," Alaina agreed.

"Yes," Grimm rumbled. "Then we hunt some hobgoblins."

Darrius' slender form swept through the foliage. Scanning the ground for signs of the hobgoblins' passing, he stopped briefly to kneel over a large indention in the earth. Examining the track, he frowned as he cast his gaze ahead. Alaina stepped up behind him, followed soon after by Divana and Halvar; who now carried a round metal shield while armored in a shiny suit of chain mail with a white surcoat and a coif to protect his head. A length of golden chain hung around his neck, bearing an emblem of a golden sun—the holy symbol of The Powers of Light.

"They're headed northwest. Hurry," Darrius instructed before continuing on again.

"Hurry up, Grimm," Divana called back as she, Alaina, and Halvar took off to follow the elven tracker. Several feet back, the panting dwarf came rushing through the underbrush.

"I'm comin' as fast as I can," he curmudgeonly replied.

Negotiating the trees around them, the group made its way up a steep hill, soon arriving at the mouth of a cave. "The trail ends here," Darrius said as Grimm finally caught up to the group. The cave's entrance reeked of offal and refuse, the stench assailing the group's nostrils as they peered inside with disgust. Setting her pack aside, Alaina dug out a torch and lit it with the flint and steel of a tinderbox. "Grimm and I should lead," Darrius suggested. "We can see in the dark."

"I could carry that," Divana said to Alaina, offering her services as torch bearer. Accepting Divana's offer, Alaina drew her sword to follow Darrius and Grimm. With Halvar and Divana watching the rear, the group entered the gaping maw of the cavern.

Creeping along, Darrius drew and readied his bow, aiming it low, yet prepared to fire in an instant. Grimm walked at his side with his axe and shield in hand. "If it wasn't for the smell, this wouldn't be so bad," Grimm whispered, as he was fully comfortable underground.

"What can you see up ahead?" Alaina asked as Darrius and Grimm paused to stare down the dark tunnel.

"Looks like it branches off up ahead." Darrius replied. "Another twenty feet or so, I'd guess."

The group pressed on until the tunnel branched off in two separate directions.

"Which way should we go?" Grimm asked as he looked to the left, then to the right.

Alaina pointed her sword down the left tunnel. "Let's try this one first," she said. "We can mark the walls with some chalk if it looks like we could get lost. I have some in the front pouch of my pack."

Holding the torch up, Divana extracted the chalk from Alaina's pack. With Darrius and Grimm still taking point, the group continued on while marking the base of the wall every so often.

The group soon came to another opening. Darrius paused while holding a hand up to halt the advance of everyone who followed. Quiet sobs and groans emanated from the opening as a fire's light flickered from beyond.

Grimm peeked inside, noticing that it opened into another chamber of the cavern. In the chamber's center, a large campfire burned. At least a dozen men, women, and even a pair of small boys were huddled together on one side of the chamber, their wrists manacled before them with strong chains. Standing over the prisoners was a trio of hobgoblins. In the hands of one was a wicked-looking whip. "Quiet, human," it ordered one frightened peasant. A crack of the whip echoed throughout the chamber as the humanoid flicked it threateningly.

"The prisoners are inside," Grimm whispered back to the others. Darrius knocked and drew an arrow, aiming it at the hobgoblin with the whip.

"Wait," Divana whispered. In unison, all in the group turned their eyes on her. "Lemme try something."

Setting the torch aside, Divana stepped up to the chamber's entrance. With her head lowered and her eyes closed, she crossed her arms before her chest, the index and little fingers of each hand extended. The hobgoblins turned to spot her as she suddenly flung out her arms.

"Alagarra Napptim."

Divana's chant echoed throughout the chamber, her hand seeming to sparkle as she pointed a finger at the targets of her spell. Darrius aimed his bow again as the hobgoblins each drew a sword and began to advance. Suddenly, their weapons slipped from their grasp to clatter upon the stone floor. Their movements began to appear sluggish as a glazed look appeared in their eyes. Eyelids began to descend as their mouths opened wide to expose sharp, pointy teeth. Slumping to their knees, the hobgoblins collapsed to the ground.

Divana entered the chamber as loud snores reverberated off the cavern walls.

"What did you do to them?" Alaina asked.

"Just a slumber spell." Divana smiled. "They shouldn't wake up for quite a while. Unfortunately, it's the only spell I have committed to my memory. I have trouble trying to remember the gestures and words to more than one at a time."

"Magic is difficult to master," Darrius said.

"We can discuss that another time," Halvar suggested. "We need to get these people out of here."

Short work was made of the prisoners' restraints soon after Divana found a key to their shackles on one of the sleeping hobgoblins. Alaina scanned the people for a girl who could possibly be the mayor's fifteen-year-old daughter. She saw none.

"We're looking for Mayor Grunswald's daughter," she announced.

One of the townsfolk, a large, bearded man in simple clothes, stepped forward.

"Those creatures took her away."

"Follows us," Halvar instructed. "We will get you folks to safety."

With the townspeople in tow, the group made its way back.

"You should get these people out of here," Halvar suggested to Divana. "We'll check this other tunnel."

Divana nodded.

"Alright, people, follow me."

As Divana led the people back to the cave's entrance, the others continued down the second tunnel. Darrius and Grimm again took the lead as Halvar and Alaina followed, each with a torch in hand.

Moments passed in tense silence as the group crept on. Suddenly, the sound of footsteps and clanking metal caught their ears. Up the tunnel ahead, a pair of shadows could be seen. Through the aid of their dark sight, Darrius and Grimm spotted a pair of the humanoids in the darkness ahead.

Growls and strange words in a language none in the group understood echoed throughout the tunnel.

"Hobgoblins!" Grimm shouted as he rushed forward.

"No...wait!" Halvar called out as the patrolling hobgoblins took off. Darrius quickly fired an arrow over his shorter companion, a loud screech following as one of the hobgoblins fell. Alaina and Halvar rushed past him, hoping to catch up with Grimm before he possibly ran into an ambush.

Grimm was soon joined by the others as he ran into another large chamber at the tunnel's end. Another opening lay at the chamber's opposite side, from which two dozen more hobgoblins emerged.

Grimm's roar of fury was deafening as he charged on. With weapons drawn, Alaina and Halvar followed the dwarf as he smashed into the first hobgoblin with his shield. Blasting through, his short, stocky form was soon lost in the horde as he waded in, swinging his axe like a madman.

The sound of clashing metal filled the cavern. Alaina and Halvar raised their shields, blocking a barrage of sword blades and spearheads. Several arrows sailed past them as Darrius fired his bow with deadly accuracy; three of the hobgoblins falling prey to the volley. Halvar bashed the head of a fourth with his mace, while Alaina's sword cut down two more.

Within the mob, Grimm managed to drop two with wild swings before a third struck the side of his head with a heavy mace. Grimm crashed hard to the ground, his metal helmet flying from his head to skid across the cold earth.

"Grimm!" Darrius shouted upon seeing his friend fall. He quickly drew another arrow, but before he could fire, a large form crashed into his side, his arrow sailing off target as a charging hobgoblin knocked him to the ground with a shoulder ram.

Darrius rolled onto his back as a large foot was planted firmly on his chest. Pinned to the ground, he found himself staring up at the hobgoblin standing over him. It held a mace high above its head in preparation for a killing blow.

Thinking quickly, Darrius drew his knife from his side, thrusting its inward-curved blade deep into the creature's calf. Howling in pain, the hobgoblin limped back as Darrius withdrew the blade and sprung to his feet. Thrusting the knife into the side of the hobgoblin's neck to finish it, he then turned and threw it into the chest of another hobgoblin as it charged him with a spear.

A dazed Grimm pushed himself to his feet as Alaina and Halvar managed to fight their way to his side, their combined efforts pushing back the remaining hobgoblins that would have otherwise finished him off while he was down. Shaking his head to clear the grogginess, Grimm suddenly noticed another hulking figure as it entered the chamber.

As it emerged from the same opening that the hobgoblin mob had come from, its heavy footfalls pounded the stone floor as it lumbered in. A low growl rumbled from the reddish-furred creature as it surveyed the ongoing skirmish with penetrating red eyes. Garbed in crude animal furs, the humanoid seemed larger than the other hobgoblins around it. It gripped a large, spiked club in its right hand.

Grimm reclaimed his axe from the ground and turned to face the creature. With a snort, it soon locked eyes on him. "C'mon over here, Gruesome," Grimm grumbled, readying his axe. "I got something fer ya." The large hobgoblin squared its shoulders. The walls of the cavern shook as it issued a thunderous roar. Grimm held his ground. "C'mon!" he yelled again, his challenge barely audible above the creature's rage.

"Grimm!" Darrius screamed. "Are you crazy?! That's the hobgoblin chieftain!"

With another furious bellow, the chieftain charged. Grimm sidestepped a mighty blow as the club descended to strike the earth, bits of stone and dust kicked up from the weapon's impact. Grimm raised his axe to strike. The chieftain moved quickly, however, following up his attack with a wild back swing. Barely managing to raise his shield in time, Grimm was launched several feet by the club's impact. Crashing hard onto the cavern floor, he slid across the chamber before slamming into one of the walls.

Seeing the chieftain advance on Grimm, Alaina quickly ducked a sword's blade before slamming into the attacking hobgoblin with her shield. Knocking the humanoid aside, she charged past to run for the chieftain. Covering Alaina's flight, Halvar brought his mace down on her foe as Darrius in turn covered his back with well-placed arrows to the sides of three more hobgoblins.

Halvar managed to reach Grimm's side. Laying his mace and shield on the ground, he laid his hands on the chest of the fallen dwarf.

"Powers of Light... restore health and vigor to our fallen comrade..."

The cleric's hands began to glow, and Grimm's eyes slowly opened. Three hobgoblins closed in as Halvar attempted to help Grimm to his feet, their efforts at attacking thwarted as Darrius rapidly fired arrows into their sides and chests.

Meanwhile, Alaina closed with the hobgoblin chieftain. With a furious cry, she leaped in as the creature turned to meet her attack. Swinging her sword, she cut a deep gash into the chieftain's left shoulder with a forehand attack. Pressing on with a back hand, she cut across the humanoid's jawbone with a glancing blow as it tried to stagger back. The chieftain glared at her. A slight trickle of red began to run from its cut jaw as it roared in anger.

Raising the club in both hands, the chieftain sent a mighty blow crashing down on Alaina's upraised shield. More blows rained down as she clenched her teeth. The impact of each blow caused her knees to buckle, with the fourth finally forcing her down to her right knee. With its left hand, the chieftain suddenly seized the top edge of her shield. With her arm stuck in the shield's straps, Alaina was sent crashing to the ground as she was flung aside. From her prone position, she looked up in horror as she had landed at the feet of another hobgoblin. An upraised axe was in its grasp.

There was a loud sizzling sound, and the hobgoblin's eyes suddenly opened wide. Letting out a wild shriek, it dropped the axe; leaping away as it grabbed at its posterior with both hands. Standing behind the creature was Divana with a torch in hand.

Seizing the opportunity to strike, Alaina quickly lunged upward, driving her sword through the hobgoblin's belly to finish it off. Getting to her feet, she gave a nod of gratitude to Divana before turning her attention back to her allies.

The remaining hobgoblins and their chieftain charged at Halvar, Darrius, and a wobbly Grimm. Darrius launched two more arrows at their enemies as Halvar stepped forward. From around his neck he removed the holy symbol, brandishing it with courage and conviction.

"Powers of Light... give us your aid in this darkest hour!"

The symbol shined with a brilliant white light. The hobgoblins shrieked as they dropped their weapons; their charge halted abruptly as they attempted to shield their eyes. Grimm charged once again, swinging his axe wildly as he cut down his blinded foes.

From behind the hobgoblin chieftain, Alaina charged in. With a cry of fury, she lunged, driving the blade of her sword through the chieftain's back. Dropping to its knees as Grimm finished off the remainder of the hobgoblins, the chieftain crashed face first to the ground.

Breathing heavily, Alaina pulled her sword from the creature's back as she looked at her allies.

"We did it," she said.

"C'mon," Halvar suggested, motioning for the others to follow him to the chamber that the hobgoblins came from. "Mayor Grunswald's daughter must be here somewhere..."

Followed by the others, Halvar entered the chamber. The light from sconces on the walls flickered and danced about the area. Large stones were positioned to form a throne-like seat at the back of the chamber, a pair of large cloth sacks at its side.

A young woman sat before the throne. Dirt and grime marred the simple white tunic and blue dress that she wore. Her wavy brown hair was disheveled as the lengthy strands cascaded over her shoulders. Her hands rested in her lap, shackled at the wrists as she looked up; her eyes alight with joy as the group hurried to her.

"Are you the mayor's daughter?" Alaina asked as Divana unlocked her restraints.

"Yes... I am Alyssa Grunswald. Thank you for saving me."

Alaina, Halvar, Darrius, and Divana all looked at one another with congratulatory glances for a hard-fought victory before noticing that Grimm was not among them. Scanning the chamber, they soon spotted him opening one of the bags beside the throne.

The dwarf's eyes shined as he cupped his hands and dipped them into the contents. A mound of silvery coins rose from his upheld palms, overflowing to rain back down with metallic chinks. He turned to look at his companions. All smiled as the dwarf's deep chuckle soon turned into a bellow of laughter.

Cheers and cries of joy greeted the group as they lead the liberated townsfolk back to Grafton, a mob of people flocking to surround them in the street. Husbands were reunited with wives and parents with children. The group tossed a glance behind them as Grimm struggled on, the two large sacks of coin that formed the bulk of the hobgoblins' treasure clearly weighing him down.

Mayor Grunswald embraced his daughter and turned to the group.

"Our town owes you heroes a great debt of gratitude," he said. "You will have the gold I promised you immediately."

From amid the mass of people, Agamemnon emerged. Beneath his beard, his mouth formed a smile. "Well done, heroes."

Breathing heavily, Grimm flopped the sacks on the ground. "Ya know what I could use right now?" he huffed.

"A drink?" Darrius guessed. The dwarf's ear-to-ear grin was evidence enough that his answer was the correct one.

"This calls for a celebration," Alaina proclaimed before turning her attention to the gathered townspeople. "Drinks are on us, everyone!"

"Hail the heroes!" a voice called out from somewhere in the crowd. The group smiled as they were surrounded once more by upraised hands and cheers of praise for their valor and bravery.

CHAPTER
2
Foe from the Past

O k," Kevin started. "You guys each get one thousand experience points for defeating the hobgoblins and rescuing the mayor's daughter. That should put you all at level two."

"Hey, does anyone else want a soda?" Josh asked while making his way toward the stairs leading back up to the kitchen.

"I'll take one," Amy said.

"Hey, bring me one, too, would ya?" Jake requested as well.

"Just bring the whole twenty-four pack of cherry cola down," Kevin suggested. "We'll wait for you to get back before we go on."

"So did I do alright?" Jennifer asked.

"You did good," Amy replied. "I think the spell you chose to memorize before we went after the hobgoblins was a good choice."

Jennifer grinned. "Well, you helped me pick it. I would have probably picked Mystic Bolt again."

Peter leaned over the table, pointing at the list of spells on Jennifer's character sheet.

"You're level two now, though," he said. "So now you learn a new spell, and you can memorize two spells at a time instead of just one."

"Also, Mystic Bolt is a spell that gets better as you level up," Kevin added. "You can fire an additional bolt for each level up to a max of five."

"Cool." Jennifer beamed. "So now I can fire two."

"Here, I'll help you pick a new spell to add to your spell book," Amy offered, while flipping through one of the game's rule books.

Josh soon returned with the box of soda, setting it beside the couch before again seating himself. "I think those cookies your mom's baking are almost done," he said as he tore open the box to begin handing out beverages.

"Yeah, she said she'd bring em down when they were done..." Kevin replied.

"Thanks," Amy said gratuitously, being the first to receive a can of soda. Her eyes met Josh's for a brief moment as her lips shaped into a warm smile.

"Dude," Jake whispered while leaning toward Josh. "I think she likes you."

Josh glanced back up at Amy while popping the top on his soda. From beneath a navy blue baseball cap, the straight strands of her long blonde hair draped over the left shoulder of the light blue t-shirt that she wore while held together in a ponytail. Despite a few freckles and her tomboyish appearance, Josh found her to be a pretty girl.

"You should ask her out," Jake continued.

"Alright," Kevin began, ready to resume the game. "After a night of celebrating and some much-needed rest, you all awaken the next morning in your rooms at the Golden Tankard Inn. You all gather at one of the tables, and after enjoying a hearty breakfast, you divide the two hundred gold pieces that the mayor gave you, along with the remaining silver from the hobgoblin's lair."

"We'll get another round of drinks while we're at it," Jake chimed in eagerly.

"Okay, anyone else who wants another mug of ale or mead has to pay two more copper coins," Kevin stated. All the players began erasing to make the necessary subtractions to the treasure on their character sheets.

"We'll get meals, too," Peter said.

"Those are two silver pieces each," Kevin replied.

"It was cool seeing my old character Agamemnon again," Josh said.

"That's your old character?" Jennifer asked in surprise.

"Yep," Kevin interjected. "All of the old group is retired from adventuring to rule over kingdoms and other things."

"Except for Amy's," Jake added with a sarcastic chuckle. Amy stuck her tongue out at him in reply.

"Anyway back to the game," Kevin said, once again declaring an interest in ending the shop talk and continuing the adventure. "You're all at the Golden Tankard dividing your treasure..."

Laughter and music from the instruments of nearby minstrels surrounded the group as they sat at a round table near the tavern's center. Grimm tilted his head back while lifting the bottom of his mug up. Streams of honey mead trickled out of the corners of his mouth as he set the empty mug aside. Belching loudly, he wiped the excess liquid from his mouth and beard with the back of his hand. "Now that's good mead." At Grimm's side, Darrius arched an eyebrow while sipping at a goblet of his own.

Seated across the table, Alaina and Divana slid empty plates aside as they watched Halvar count the coins. Dividing them into equal portions, he slid one stack of gold and eight stacks of silver to each at the table, ensuring that the mayor's payment and the spoils of last night's skirmish were evenly distributed.

"Alright... that's forty gold and four hundred silver for each of us..."

"Sounds fair to me," Alaina agreed as all claimed their share.

"There would be twice as much if you hadn't decided to treat the town to drinks last night," Grimm complained.

Alaina looked at Grimm in annoyance.

"And just what do you have to spend gold on that is soooo important?" she retorted.

Darrius grinned.

"He just drank it."

Grimm roared with laughter before he turned to wave for one of the tavern's serving girls. "Hey... another mead over here!" he bellowed.

"Isn't that his third drink?" Divana asked as a serving girl placed another frothy mug before the dwarf.

"Yes, I believe so," Halvar replied.

Grimm placed two copper coins in the young, dark-haired woman's palm. As she turned to leave, he quickly smacked her on the derriere with an open hand, a shriek erupting from her as she tossed eye daggers at the offending dwarf. "Odious beast," she mumbled while storming away. Alaina arched an eyebrow at Darrius as though looking for an explanation for such barbaric behavior. Darrius only shrugged his shoulders.

"Such behavior may bring you trouble one day," Halvar warned.

"From the stories I've heard, it got his father into trouble on many occasions," Darrius said.

Grimm offered no reply to the comments, as his only concern seemed to be the golden beverage before him. An ear-to-ear grin formed beneath his heavy beard. His eyes shined like gems as he lifted the foam-crowned mug to his mouth and slowly began to raise its bottom up.

"Hey, it's Agamemnon," Divana suddenly said, nodding to the tavern entrance. All at the table turned their attention to the elderly, bearded wizard who stood in the doorway. With his gnarled staff in hand, he began to make his way through the people. His green robes flowed as he approached the group's table, a grave expression peeking out from beneath his hat.

"Speaking of trouble..." Halvar frowned. "I'm not sure I like the looks of this."

The wizard stopped before them.

"You must come with me at once."

"What is the trouble?" Alaina asked.

Agamemnon's eyes narrowed. "Follow me to Illingrad," he replied. "I shall explain everything there."

"Illingrad's only a couple of miles from Grafton, isn't it?" Josh asked.

Kevin nodded. "Yep, two miles to the west."

"We'll gather our things and follow Agamemnon," Amy declared.

"Damn, I just got this beer," Jake complained in character.

"You all quickly gather your gear and follow Agamemnon," Kevin continued after a quick smirk to Jake. "The trip is pretty calm as you walk along the road, and you make it to Illingrad in about half an hour or so." The structures in the town pretty much look the same as they did in Grafton. Continuing along the dirt road through the town, you eventually come to a tall tower of gray stone..."

"I didn't even get to finish my drink," Grimm grumbled as the group followed Agamemnon through the wooden door that served as the tower's entrance.

"You've been complaining about that all the way here," Darrius said as the group crossed the floor of a large circular chamber, passing around the skeleton of an enormous dragon that was erected at its center.

"Yeah, give it a rest, for pity's sake," Alaina agreed as she and the others continued to follow Agamemnon, who had begun ascending a winding stone stairway that hugged the chamber's walls. At the stairway's apex stood another sturdy wooden door. Its hinges creaked and groaned as Agamemnon pushed it open and strode through.

The group followed behind to enter another large circular chamber. Shelves lined with tomes of varying sizes and volumes covered the walls. At the opposite end of the chamber was a large, ovular portal which allowed a view of the hilly countryside far below. In the center of the room's stone floor rested a large pedestal of bronze, its shape taking the likeness of a mighty dragon claw. Held up within its grasp was a crystal sphere, its diameter roughly thrice that of a human skull.

Agamemnon stepped before the crystal ball. Casually, he waved a hand over the sphere, and a dim white light soon afterward shone within it.

"What is it that you need from us?" Halvar asked.

Agamemnon stepped aside, while gesturing toward the crystal ball. Halvar and the others gathered around the globe as an image began to slowly appear within its thick, glassy confines.

Along the length of a corridor's stone walls ran a group of four. Torches along the walls cast a soft orange glow about the otherwise dark hall, lighting the way for the group in their seemingly urgent haste.

A stout-looking dwarf with a thick, flame-red beard was clad in a chain mail shirt and hefting a heavy maul in his hands. The lithe, tan-and-green-clad form of an elf ran along a few feet ahead of him, long blonde hair trailing behind him as he rushed on. A long sword was held in his right hand and a short sword in his left.

"Darrius... look!" Grimm whispered in astonishment while pointing to the events that unfolded within the crystal ball.

"Our fathers..." Darrius quietly stated.

Agamemnon grinned in a brief moment of fond recollection.

"Yes... Ulfgar Ironforge and Ahiramil Goldleaf... two of my closest companions."

Alongside the dwarf and elf was a slender woman. Garbed in a tan leather vest with black leggings and boots, she wielded a dagger in each gloved hand. Strands of jet-black hair peeked out from beneath a crimson-red hood, and a matching cloak trailed behind in her flight. Leading the charge was a man in flowing green robes. Long strands of pale blonde hair hung to his shoulders as he cast a determined gaze down the corridor. "Hurry!" he commanded while aiming a staff of gnarled wood toward a pair of large iron doors at the corridor's end. All that were gathered around the crystal ball immediately recognized Agamemnon in his prime.

With a frown, Halvar turned to Agamemnon.

"What are we witnessing here?"

"Thirty years have passed since this battle took place," Agamemnon answered somberly. "The battle with Veros..."

"Who's Veros?" Alaina asked.

"A powerful sorcerer," Darrius interjected. "My father spoke of him before."

Grimm nodded.

"As did mine," he added somberly.

"Veros and I were apprentices to the same master," Agamemnon continued. "The master banned him from further teachings once he caught him practicing necromancy, which he had strictly forbidden."

"Necromancy?" Alaina asked.

"Magic that deals with the dead," Divana offered.

"After his exile, he disappeared for many a year," Agamemnon continued, turning his attention briefly to the group. "I adventured with my companions and continued my quest to master the arcane arts, even after my master had passed on. Then one day there was an attack on the city in which the magic school was."

"What kind of attack?" Halvar inquired.

"Creatures neither living nor dead came from the city's grave sites to attack the living," Agamemnon said. "Some of them were merely skeletal remains, while others were rotting horrors to behold. Despite my best efforts, the city was destroyed. I discovered that this was occurring all over Urith's lands and soon learned that Veros had mastered his macabre sorcery, but that wasn't the worst of it."

Alaina frowned. "Go on..."

"Veros had somehow created a mighty rod," Agamemnon continued, dread etched on his visage. "One with the power to reanimate the dead anywhere in the world. Corpses rose by the legion to do his bidding as he amassed an army of death. After many a tribulation, my allies and I managed to finally reach his stronghold." Agamemnon returned his attention to the crystal ball and the scene playing out within.

"And the battle to follow was terrible to behold..."

The end of Agamemnon's staff glowed with a fiery light. The doors at the corridor's end burst open, swinging inward with tremendous force as the wizard and his allies charged in. A large, circular chamber greeted them, the ceiling high above hidden by darkness as the heroes readied themselves for battle.

Standing before them, and numbering too many to count, was a horde of creatures which were apparently no longer among the living. Many were mere skeletons, clad in tattered rags and incomplete armor. Red pinpoints of light burned in hollow eye sockets as they wielded rusty swords and axes. Others were seemingly mindless, slow-moving corpses that shambled about clothed in mere tattered rags while in varying stages of decomposition.

Flames rose from a pair of large pits in the middle of the chamber's stone floor. Between the pillars of fire, a flight of stone steps could be seen at the back of the chamber. At the stairway's apex sat a throne which seemed to be constructed from human bones.

Seated upon the ghastly chair was a pale man in black robes. The light of the fire pit reflected off of his eyes, giving the figure a nigh-demonic look. His bald head was covered in tattoos of strange, arcane symbols. A black goatee on his chin tapered to a point.

Slowly, the dark-robed figure stood. Grasped firmly in his right hand was a length of ivory in the likeness of a human femur. Strange symbols adorned the length of the grisly-looking rod and a chunk of black obsidian was set firmly in one end of it. He pointed an index finger which ended with a long cracked nail at the heroes.

"You and your companions should not have come, Agamemnon." Veros hissed. "There is nothing for you here but death."

Agamemnon and the others held their ground.

"Your annihilation will only strengthen my forces, for in death I will be your master." Veros proclaimed while leveling the rod. "Destroy them!"

At the necromancer's command, the undead mob began to advance.

Ulfgar's furious roar echoed throughout the chamber as the group charged to meet Veros' undead minions head on. Like a barroom brawler, the dwarf waded into the thick of the skeletons, his heavy maul blasting several of them apart as he attacked with mighty swings.

Ahiramil swiftly moved to protect Ulfgar's rear. Parrying a rusty sword blade with his own long sword, he drove his short sword through the skeleton's ribs with an upward lunge that broke the ribcage apart. Raising the long sword, he brought it down to crush another skeleton as he hacked through its brittle collarbone and ribcage.

A blow from Agamemnon's staff shattered the jaw of yet another one as he looked to the red-cloaked woman who was also his ally. With the grace and agility of a cat, she bravely engaged a horde of skeletons: evading their weapons with flips and somersaults while smashing them with well-placed elbows and martial art-style kicks. "Behind you, Dagger!" Agamemnon warned the woman as a group of shambling corpses began to close in behind her.

Quickly pivoting, Dagger ducked a pair of rotting, outstretched arms while plunging the dagger in her left hand into the gut of the decaying zombie. Bringing her right hand up and around, she executed a back hand swing with the other knife to cut across the throat of the zombie, its head coming off to hit the floor with a series of sickening thuds.

She executed a diving roll toward two more of the walking corpses. Rolling over her right shoulder, she came up to rest on her left knee as she simultaneously thrust a blade into each of the creatures' stomachs before quickly dashing past them to engage yet another one. With a leaping kick, she knocked the zombie onto its back before lunging to stab a blade into the prone creature's neck.

Veros began a descent down the steps. Slowly, he raised the rod, aiming it toward the ensuing battle below. A dull nimbus of light surrounded the large shard of obsidian that was embedded in the rod's end. The bones of previously vanquished skeletons that lay inert upon the floor soon began to tremble. Rolling and sliding into place, they suddenly erected to assemble into whole skeletons once more.

"They're reanimating!" Ahiramil screamed while beheading a zombie with his long sword.

Agamemnon thrust the end of his staff forward, knocking back an incoming zombie. "It's the rod!" he observed. "We have to destroy the rod!"

Ulfgar shattered the legs of another zombie with a blow from his maul before bringing it down on the creature's head to finish it off. "I'll get it!" he shouted.

"Ulfgar!" Ahirimil screamed. "No!"

With a bellow of rage, Ulfgar blasted through several zombies and skeletons with horizontal swings of his hammer. Soon clearing a path, he unleashed a second roar, charging for Veros as the necromancer reached the base of the steps.

With a cruel smirk, Veros continued to advance. Nonchalantly raising his left hand, he aimed its palm and fingers toward the charging dwarf. "Morketh Al Neirakarr," he hissed.

A vaporous mass began to coalesce around his hand, forming misty tendrils as they snaked forth. Suddenly, the tendrils took the shape of a large phantom hand as they shot toward Ulfgar. The hand's fingers wrapped tightly around the dwarf's upper body, the maul falling from his grasp as he was launched to slide several feet across the stone floor. Ulfgar's head poked out between the index and middle fingers of the hand as the other two fingers and thumb wrapped around his torso to maintain a vice-like grip.

Grasping desperately at the fingers, Ulfgar tried to pull himself free of the hand as Veros strode between the two fire pits. With a malice-filled glare, he began to gradually curl the fingers of his upheld hand inward, as though he were crushing something within his grasp. Ulfgar's face contorted in pain as the phantom fingers began to constrict him.

Agamemnon swung his staff wildly as he attempted to keep the horde of undead at bay, smashing nearly a dozen skeletons. As Ahiramil and Dagger slashed and stabbed at zombies, he quickly flung an open palm toward the hand that held Ulfgar.

"Aldaroth!"

Lying flat on his back, Ulfgar gasped for air as Veros' magic was dispelled. Rage twisted the necromancer's face, his nostrils flaring as he turned his gaze toward Agamemnon.

"You..."

Quickening his pace, Veros resumed his stride, walking with purpose as he headed straight for Agamemnon. Raising the rod in both hands, he swung it downward as Agamemnon brought his staff up to block the descending strike. Veros suddenly lashed out with his right leg, slamming a heel into Agamemnon's gut to send him sprawling onto his back.

Seeing Agamemnon fall, Ahiramil and Dagger fought with renewed vigor. Dodging around a zombie's outstretched arms, Dagger sliced into its triceps before dropping to plunge a knife deep into its groin. Pivoting away, she then executed a diving roll past four more corpses. Ahiramil followed behind her with several sword slashes and kicks to decapitate or knock the undead back.

Crawling across the floor, Ulfgar managed to reclaim his maul and struggle to his feet once more. Reentering the fray, he slammed the hammer into two more zombies before ducking a skeleton's axe. Dagger rushed in, leaping over the dwarf to smash and splinter the skeleton's ribs with a well-placed jump kick. Continuing her flight, she dodged around three more skeletons. Ulfgar protected her rear, smashing the skeletons as Ahiramil joined him to fight back-to-back.

With her path clear, Dagger rushed for Veros, who stalked a prone Agamemnon but a few feet away. Again Veros lifted the rod to strike, stopping as he caught sight of Dagger out of the corner of his eye.

"You thieves... Always trying to stab someone in the back, aren't you?"

Veros turned toward Dagger, bringing the rod around with a back hand swing. Springing off both legs, Dagger leaped into the air, flipping over Veros as his attack passed harmlessly beneath her. Landing behind him, she tucked and rolled to absorb the impact of her landing before diving away. Twisting to face him in midair, Dagger threw both her knives.

Veros spun around in time for the first blade to stab deep into his left shoulder. A scream of pain erupted from him as the second dagger struck the rod, knocking it from his grasp to slide across the floor several feet away.

Landing on her back, Dagger quickly tucked her legs. With her elbows up, she pressed her palms to the floor beside her head before kicking out with her legs to spring back to her feet. Her red cloak flared behind her as she again charged Veros, who clenched his teeth in pain while yanking the blade out of his shoulder. Leaping through the air, Dagger blasted Veros with a jump kick. The heel of her foot slammed hard into his sternum to send him crashing onto his back, the blade he had pulled from his flesh landing to clatter at her feet.

Ulfgar and Ahiramil continued to fight back-to-back, finally defeating the remnants of the undead horde with continual parries, slashes, and strikes. Pushing himself up to his hands and knees, Agamemnon watched as Dagger picked up the blade and began moving toward Veros. Stepping up to his prone body, she seized him by the front of his robes, jerking him to his knees as she drew the knife back for the kill.

Veros suddenly grabbed Dagger's wrist with his right hand. His eyes shined with hate as he stared up at her. Dagger froze, her eyes widening. Maintaining his hold, Veros slowly stood. A wicked grin stretched across his face as Dagger's weapon slipped from her grasp. Agamemnon's eyes widened in horror.

No...

Dagger began to gasp for air, clutching at her chest with her free hand. Her flesh began to wrinkle and sag as she visibly began to age, the toll of decades seeming to pass in mere seconds as her clothing loosened. Her flesh and hair shriveled as her eyes sank in, the decomposition process seeming to flash by. Within seconds, she was but a skeleton, soon after crumbling to dust.

Veros smiled, while casually dusting off his hands. Agamemnon's scream reverberated throughout the chamber, his hand reaching out in desperate futility for his fallen comrade.

"No!"

Agamemnon jumped to his feet. With another scream of rage, he flung his right arm back, a ball of flame suddenly appearing in his open palm.

"Arrigoss Luminoss!"

Veros turned his gaze to Agamemnon, a smirk forming as the wizard's wrath was unleashed. The chamber's walls shook from the fireball's explosion, Veros' form lost within the inferno. Joined by Ulfgar and Ahiramil, Agamemnon approached the spot where Veros had stood as the smoke cleared. Only the scorched stone floor remained. There was no trace of the necromancer, save the remnants of his undead minions and the rod.

Halvar frowned at the battle's conclusion.

"By The Powers..."

"Dagger was lost on that fateful day," Agamemnon lamented as the image within the crystal ball faded. "I suspect that Veros somehow escaped. At the battle's conclusion, I claimed his rod to prevent it from ever again falling into his evil hands."

There was a brief bout of silence.

"So what is it that you need from us?" Alaina finally asked.

Agamemnon waved his hand over the crystal ball once more. The stone walls of a small chamber appeared. A lone pedestal of ornate bronze sat in its center. Its rectangular shape suggested that it was constructed to hold something of fair length, its likeness made into that of a pair of talons that were erected from its altar-like surface. The open claws sat silent and empty. Agamemnon breathed a deep sigh.

"The Rod of Veros is gone."

Divana gasped.

"Gone?!"

"My young apprentice, Jerrod, is missing as well," Agamemnon continued. "I suspect that he has taken the rod."

"But why would Jerrod take the rod?" Divana asked in surprise.

Agamemnon frowned. "I suspect a darker force is at work here, manipulating events from afar."

"You mean..." Halvar started.

"Yes." Agamemnon nodded. "Veros has returned."

"So what would you have us do?" Darrius asked.

"And how much are we being paid for this?" Grimm added.

Alaina frowned at the dwarf's greed. "There are more important things than gold, you know..."

Agamemnon waved his hand over the crystal ball again. This time, however, only a billowing mass of fog-like vapor could be seen; no image formed within the sphere.

"It is my belief that the attack of the hobgoblins on Grafton yesterday was but a diversion to draw my attention elsewhere while Jerrod stole the rod," he said. "I know not how my pupil is being manipulated, but I think Veros is protecting him from any magic that would reveal his location, as I cannot seem to scry on him. You must find Jerrod and recover the Rod of Veros."

"So where do we start looking?" Halvar asked, his conviction to oppose the forces of darkness clearly evident. Agamemnon stared off for a moment as though pondering something. "Jerrod will need supplies," he mused. "Korringlenn is the closest major city, about two days' ride northeast of here. That is probably where he is headed."

"Then we should get ourselves some horses and get going," Alaina quickly suggested.

"Be careful on your journey," Agamemnon warned. "There has been talk of goblins in the woods, and Korringlenn itself has its own dangers. Divana shall accompany you again, as her magic should prove an asset." Divana nodded in quiet agreement as Agamemnon placed a hand upon her shoulder.

"Very well," Halvar said. "Let us make haste."

With that, the group turned to leave. "Ok," Grimm started. "But how much are we getting paid?"

"Are you kidding me?!" Jake cried. "Veros again?!"

Kevin grinned in quiet reply.

"Told you he teleported," Peter said.

All at the table suddenly turned their attention to the sound of footfalls on the basement stairs. The folds of a long white skirt descended into view as the soles of tan leather loafers thumped against the wooden steps.

"Cookies are ready, kids," Mrs. Mckanahan said, setting a plate of cookies in the center of the table.

Kevin smiled. "Thanks, Mom..."

"Chocolate chip," Josh said, reaching for the plate. "My favorite."

Picking up one of the cookies, he suddenly gasped in surprise. Fumbling the cookie, he dropped it across his chest and into his lap, the chocolate leaving a few small stains across the front of his clean green-and-white baseball tee.

"Oh! Oh! Hot," he said.

Amy smiled as she and the others each claimed a cookie for themselves.

"Easy there, tiger," she said, giggling.

Josh smiled sheepishly, a twinge of embarrassment coursing through him as he picked up the cookie and blew on it a few times in an attempt to cool it off for consumption. Amy smiled, amused by his antics.

"Your father and I will be going out soon, so behave yourselves while we're gone," Mrs. Mckanahan teased.

"Yeah, sure, Mom," Kevin replied with a smirk.

"Thank you for the cookies, Mrs. Mckanahan," Amy said, with the others around the table remembering their manners and expressing gratitude soon afterward.

Mrs. Mckanahan smiled.

"You're welcome. There's another batch upstairs. There's also another twenty-four pack of cola and some pizzas in the freezer, if you all want those. You kids have fun."

With that, Kevin's mother made her way back upstairs as the youths continued to munch on the moist cookies.

"Ok," Jennifer started. "We all need to get horses?"

"Yep," Kevin replied. "Unless you wanna walk, and I wouldn't recommend it, since you guys are in a hurry. Jerrod already has a head start on you."

"I hate horses." Jake said, roleplaying Grimm's weariness of the creatures.

"Well, you'll just have to get over it," Amy said, as Alaina would have if given a similar complaint.

Behind his screen, Kevin flipped through the pages of one of the game's books. "Horses, along with the saddles and all, will cost you guys thirty gold each."

"I'm gonna buy a pony," Jake declared.

"That'll be ten gold pieces," Kevin replied as everyone subtracted the amount from their listed treasure.

"That should be about all we need," Josh stated. "We'll fill our wineskins with water and go after Jerrod."

"Can I hit him with Mystic Bolt when we see him?" Jennifer asked.

Amy grinned. "Might not be a bad idea," she said.

"Alright," Kevin interjected. "With your horses..." He paused, tossing a grin to Jake before continuing. "And your pony, you set out on your two-day ride, passing through Grafton again as you head to Korringlenn..."

Chapter
3
Attack of the Goblins

Lush trees and bushes dotted the area on both sides of the quiet dirt road. Clouds of dust were kicked up by the hooves of the group's steeds as they galloped along. Darrius and Halvar's horses took the lead as they ran side by side. Alaina and Divana followed close behind them as Grimm's pony brought up the rear several feet back. The sun had begun to set behind the distant hills as the sky's brightness slowly faded. The group brought their mounts to a halt.

Darrius looked to the sky.

"It'll be dark soon... another hour, maybe."

"We should find a spot near the road and make camp," Alaina suggested.

"Agreed." Halvar nodded. "We'll continue on at first light."

The chirping of crickets rang throughout the forest. A few yards from the road, the campfire's light was brilliant in the darkness. With the erected tents of the group at her back, Divana sat quietly on the ground, looking over a small tome in her lap that was her spell book. Kneeling beside her, Halvar stoked the fire with a stick, clad in the more comfortable robes of his order rather than the heavy armor of his chain shirt and coif.

Alaina and Grimm soon approached, their arms loaded with as much firewood as they could find and carry from near the camp.

"There," Alaina said as she and Grimm dropped their loads into a pile. "This should get us through the night."

Seating himself upon the ground, Grimm began sharpening his axe with a whetstone.

"Darrius still hunting?" he asked.

"Dinner is served," a familiar voice proclaimed from the woods nearby. All in the camp turned toward Darrius as he hefted six of rabbits by their rear legs. "Just give me a moment to prepare these..."

Having memorized her spells, Divana closed her spell book and returned it to its leather pouch. "I'll give you a hand," she offered while standing to follow Darrius.

Tossing a few small sticks into the fire to keep it burning, Alaina seated herself next to Halvar. Taking a moment to warm her hands over the fire, she smiled at the priest. Glancing to her, Halvar returned the smile with one of his own, a smile that soon faded as his gaze lowered to rest upon the hilt of the blade that was sheathed at her side. "You're pretty good with that sword," he commented after a moment of pause.

Alaina turned to stare into the fire once more, her smile fading as she continued the conversation. "I was trained by my father when I was young, before war claimed his life."

Halvar's eyes softened. "I am sorry for your loss."

Alaina returned her attention to the priest, grinning slightly at his compassion.

"So how long have you been with the priesthood?" she asked after another bout of silence.

Halvar grinned.

"I joined the clergy when I was fifteen."

A long, mournful howl interrupted the conversation as all around the campfire turned toward the distant sound.

"It's a wolf," Divana observed.

Grimm stood with his axe, walking away from the campfire as he stared into the darkness beyond the campsite. Grabbing his bow, Darrius joined his side. All within the camp looked around as they suddenly noticed that the chirping of the crickets had ceased.

Beside the fire, Halvar and Alaina stood as Divana stepped up beside them.

"We should move away from the fire, too," Alaina said. "Makes us an easy target for whatever is amiss."

Her suggestion was followed by the others as all stared at the darkness beyond the camp. Growls and snarls echoed menacingly in the distance.

"What is that?" Divana whispered in concern.

Darrius suddenly launched an arrow into the darkness, his night vision allowing him to make out his target. A loud shriek followed the shot as the growls grew louder. The sound of cracking bark and trampled foliage rang out through the woods as large shapes could soon be seen.

Grimm frowned as he saw the small humanoids that rode in on large gray wolves. "Goblins."

"Wolf riders," Darrius added.

Nearing the light of the fire, the creatures became more visible. Clad in soiled greens and browns, the short, reddish-skinned creatures brandished short bladed swords and small wooden shields as their wolves charged in. Bright yellow eyes glared from flat faces, foreheads sloping from beneath rusty metal caps. Sharp little fangs lined their wide mouths as they released high-pitched shrieks and growls.

Divana let out a cry of fright as she stumbled backward, Alaina shouldering past her with her sword and shield ready. "Move, girl!" she yelled as Halvar hefted his mace.

Grimm stared down a single wolf-mounted goblin as it charged straight toward him.

"You know what I hate about goblins, Darrius?" he asked as the elf launched a volley of arrows from his side.

"What's that?" Darrius inquired.

Grimm raised his axe.

"The damn smell!" he bellowed while charging.

Lifting his shield, Grimm blocked the downward thrust of the goblin's blade. Pivoting quickly, he swung his axe, cutting a vicious wound in its mount's side. The wolf let out a pitiful yelp as it toppled over, the goblin rider shrieking loudly before being crushed beneath its weight.

Grimm held his ground as more of the wolf riders charged in. An arrow sailed past him from behind, another goblin dropping as Darrius reached for a second arrow. Under the elf's continued cover fire, Grimm pressed his attack, his axe dropping four more of the wolf riders with powerful forehand and backhand slashes.

Closer to the campfire, Alaina raised her shield to ward off the fangs of a charging wolf. With a twirling motion, she hopped to the wolf's flank as it crashed into the shield while parrying a thrust of its goblin rider's blade with her long sword. With a fierce cry, Alaina brought the sword back across, launching the goblin from its mount as she slashed the small humanoid across its chest.

At her back, Halvar brought his mace down on the wolf's head, a yelp from the creature signaling its demise as Divana seized a stick of burning wood from the fire. Turning to face several more of the creatures, Divana thrust the burning log at them in hopes of holding them at bay. "There's so many of them!" she shrieked.

Halvar raised his mace, erecting it above his head.

"Powers of Light, drive back these minions of darkness!"

The mace suddenly began to glow in the priest's hand, and a brilliant white light burst from the weapon to illuminate the area around him. Shrieks and howls of pain erupted from the blinded goblins, many of them falling from their mounts as they desperately attempted to shield their burning eyes. The creatures began to blindly stumble and crawl away as the light continued to shine, with even Alaina and Divana feeling a need to shield their eyes.

"Return to the night from whence you came, odious beasts," Halvar boldly commanded, knowing of the creatures' preference for nocturnal activity.

Alaina and Divana watched as the goblins and wolves fell back, with Grimm's axe and Darrius' bow ensuring that their retreat continued. The light from Halvar's mace soon faded, and within moments the night was still once more.

"Do you think they'll be back?" Divana asked in concern.

Turning, Alaina sheathed her sword. "Let's hope not."

"We should sleep in shifts nevertheless," Darrius suggested as Grimm only grunted in accordance. "Just in case they should return."

"Very well." Halvar nodded. "Why don't you and Grimm take first watch?"

Grimm and Darrius nodded as Halvar continued.

"Let's try and get some rest. We still have another day of riding ahead of us."

CHAPTER
4
Den of Thieves

A fter resting through the night, you all break camp and
continue on your way," Kevin said.

Glancing down, he rolled some dice behind his screen.

"You guys don't run into any more trouble during the rest
of the trip to Korringlenn."

"That's good." Amy grinned.

"How late is it when we reach the city?" Josh asked.

Kevin rolled a few more dice.

"Well, you guys made good time. It's near sundown when
you get there... about another hour or so of light left, though."

"Alright," Josh replied. "We'll all get rooms at the inn for
a night and then start lookin for Agamemnon's apprentice, ask
around and see if anyone's seen... what's his name again?"

"Jerrod," Amy interjected while holding up her character
sheet. "I wrote his name down."

"So you guys are getting rooms for the night?" Kevin asked.

"Yeah," Amy replied. "I'll approach some of the townsfolk and ask them to direct us to food and lodgings for a night."

"You'll find the Blazing Hearth just down that way," the tall, lean man in simple clothing said. He pointed an index finger down the road to further indicate the direction of the inn.

"Thank you." Alaina smiled.

The group led their mounts along the busy street. Buildings of gray and white stone were all around, many seeming to be well-maintained with tiled roofs. After several yards, they arrived at a white building; a sign above the door displaying a blazing fire within the confines of a brick hearth.

"The Blazing Hearth Inn," Halvar said, able to read the words at the sign's bottom.

Tethering his pony, Grimm rushed for the door, the sounds of laughter emanating from within the dwelling.

"Beer at last!"

Alaina sighed as Halvar turned to Darrius.

"Stay with Grimm and see if any of the inn's patrons have seen anyone matching Jerrod's description."

Darrius smiled.

"Sure. I'll see about getting us some lodgings as well."

Halvar nodded as Darrius proceeded to enter the inn.

"I'll see if I can find a temple to the Powers of Light here. Maybe some of the priests there can help us out."

Divana turned to Alaina. "We can look around and ask some more of the locals too."

Alaina nodded. "Agreed. Let's all meet back here in an hour or so with our findings."

"Ok," Kevin started. "You guys go your separate ways to conduct your investigation. Josh, Halvar finds the temple with little difficulty."

"Cool," Josh replied. "I'll spend a moment at prayer, tithe a few gold pieces, and ask some of the priests if they have heard or seen anything of Jerrod."

"Fair enough." Kevin nodded. "Darrius and Grimm are at the inn asking the patrons and barkeep, and Alaina and Divana are asking around on the street."

"Right," Amy said. Kevin rolled a few dice. With a grin, he turned to his sister Jennifer...

"I'm sorry, miss, afraid I haven't seen a lad fittin' that description."

Divana sighed.

"I see... well, thank you for your time, mister."

With a nod of his head, the stocky man in a plain shirt and trousers went on with his business. Divana turned toward Alaina, who spoke inaudibly to a well-dressed man and woman a few yards down the street.

Hope she's having better luck than me...

Suddenly, Divana felt something bump into her. Whirling, she spotted a lone figure; the individual's form hidden beneath a green cloak and hood. With a frown, she watched as the man hurried past.

How rude...

As she returned her attention to Alaina, her eyes suddenly widened. Glancing down, she suddenly noticed that her coin pouch was missing from her belt. Her eyes darted back to the cloaked figure that had bumped into her, who was now several yards away.

"Hey!"

The hooded figure glanced over his shoulder before suddenly breaking into a run.

"Come back here, you thief!" Divana yelled as she charged after him.

Moving swiftly, the figure darted amid the masses and into an alleyway to his right. Divana continued the chase. Walls of gray brick encased her on both sides as garbage littered the pathway. On she ran before coming to a dead end at another stone wall. Before the wall, the cloaked figure stood. .

"Give me back my money," Divana demanded, her mind wandering to the Mystic Bolt spell in the event that the thief should attack.

The hooded figure slowly turned. Much of his visage and form remained hidden beneath his clothing. Divana's eyes widened as a short sword was produced from beneath the cloak's folds.

"Foolish girl," a raspy voice hissed from beneath the hood.

Divana's attention snagged on the sound of footsteps at her back. Glancing over her shoulder, she spotted five more figures. The form of each was veiled in a manner similar to the individual she had chased into the alley. Her eyes widened in fear as she came to a startling realization. She had been led into a trap.

Oh, no...

More blades were drawn. The six hooded figures began to advance menacingly. Fear gripped Divana as she whirled about, frantically searching for a means of escape.

A furious cry blasted the stillness as two of the thieves suddenly sprawled forward, Alaina's shield slamming into their backs to send them face first to the ground. With Divana barely managing to scramble clear of the chaos, Alaina charged on, following her shield check with a flurry of slashes from her sword. One of the thieves received a cut across the arm as the others leaped back to avoid the onslaught. "Run, Divana!" Alaina screamed. "Find the others!"

Divana's eyes darted from the alley's entrance back to the battle as uncertainty gripped her. Alaina raised her shield, blocking a thrown dagger, which bounced off the metallic surface to clatter to the ground. With her sword, she parried the thrust of another of the thieves, the cloaked figure proving his nimbleness as he executed a back flip to avoid a return slash.

"Go!" Alaina urged again.

Reluctance seized Divana. Uncertain of what she should do, she watched in horror as four of the figures maneuvered to surround Alaina. A fifth remained slumped against the wall, still clutching at the laceration in his arm from Alaina's blade as blood stained his cloak. Divana gasped as the sixth suddenly turned his attention to her. In a flash, the cloaked figure charged, his blade drawn.

Panicked, Divana flung out her arm.

"Arrak Alabarr!"

The crackling Mystic Bolt flew from her fingertips, a cry of agony escaping the thief as he flew back. Flung from his grasp in his demise, the thief's short sword landed with a clatter at Divana's feet as she stepped back from the grisly sight. Divana looked up in alarm as she suddenly heard a cry of pain.

Alaina!

All was silent as the battle ceased. Alaina remained in the center of her foes. None moved. Seconds passed as Divana watched, perplexed by what was transpiring. Gradually, Alaina's sword and shield slipped from her grasp, the sharp clatter startling Divana as the stillness of the scene set in. A gasp escaped her as she noticed the thief by the wall, a slender tube held to his lips. In horror she suddenly noticed the small needle sticking in the side of Alaina's leg.

No!

Alaina slowly dropped to her knees, her arms hanging limp at her sides. She stared at Divana, her eyelids beginning to flutter as though heavy. "Go..." she managed to implore one final time, the needle apparently coated with some sort of sedative as she slumped to the ground unconscious.

At fear's command, Divana turned and fled. With as much speed as she could muster, she ran from the alleyway, her cries for help resounding throughout the city streets as the last vestiges of the sun soon left with the arrival of night.

Jake's laughter reverberated throughout the basement.

"Oh, my God, Amy!" he cried out. "You got captured!"

Jake's laughter continued as Amy stared at him in annoyance.

"Are you done?"

Jake's eyes began to tear up as he doubled over on the couch, the volume of his laughter beginning to die down as he held his sides.

"Oh, God, it hurts..."

Crossing her arms, Amy turned to Kevin. "Why is it that my characters always get captured?"

Kevin held up his hands in defense. "Hey, I just rolled the dice to see who the thieves went after. My sister got the lowest role, so they targeted her. It was your decision to play at being a hero while she escaped."

Amy arched an eyebrow. "Oh, sure, like I'd just let them take her away."

"Was Dagger ever captured?" Jennifer asked.

"Plenty of times," Amy replied. "She had the escape skill, though, so she was usually able to get away from her captors. My wizard I played before that, on the other hand, was always having to be rescued."

Jake snickered with seemingly fond recollection.

"Oh, yeah... Xandra... those were fun times..."

"I'm sorry, Amy," Jennifer offered apologetically.

Amy sighed. "It's ok. It's not your fault."

"Do I find Divana while I'm going to or coming back from the temple?" Josh asked anxiously.

Amy looked at Josh, her lips shaping into a smile at his eagerness to come to her rescue.

I guess chivalry isn't dead after all...

Kevin rolled some dice.

"No, you don't, nor have any of the priests seen anyone resembling Jerrod. You do overhear some talk about a rash of thefts being committed throughout the city, though. Grimm and Darrius likewise come up empty-handed. You do secure rooms for the night, however, which are a gold piece each."

"That's cool," Jake grinned. "I'm just here for the beer."

"Josh," Kevin continued. "Halvar meets back up with Darrius and Grimm at the Blazing Hearth."

Josh turned to Peter, roleplaying his character. "Find anything?"

Peter shook his head, continuing the in-character dialogue. "No one here has seen anyone matching Jerrod's description."

Josh sighed. "Barkeep hasn't seen 'em, either," Jake offered, temporarily gruffing up his voice to resemble his dwarf's before speaking normally again to narrate an action of his character. "I hold up my beer mug..."

"Suddenly," Kevin interjected, "you all see Divana burst into the inn. A look of barely-restrained panic is in her eyes as she looks about frantically." Kevin turned to Jennifer before continuing. "Divana, you spot the party standing near the bar."

All at the table turned to Jennifer, awaiting her response to Kevin's narration.

"Ok, I run over to them. I just say what my character would say, right?"

"That's right." Amy grinned.

"Ok..." Jennifer started. "Help! Alaina's in trouble!"

Peter gave Jennifer an approving thumbs up. "Not bad."

Josh frowned, keeping to his role as Halvar. "What happened?" he asked.

"Hurry!" Jennifer replied. "I'm gonna lead them back to the alley where we fought the cloaked-and-hooded guys."

"We'll follow her," Peter added.

"Alright, you all follow Divana as she takes you back to the alley where she last saw Alaina with the thieves," Kevin said before turning his attention to Amy. "Meanwhile..."

Alaina's eyes slowly fluttered open, a low moan seeping from her as she began to regain consciousness.

Where... where am I?

Her eyes darted about as she tried to get a bearing on her surroundings. All in the area was dark, save for a small amount of light that flickered off the surrounding stone walls from an oil lamp that sat on a small table in a corner of the room. Across the way next to the table was a sturdy-looking wooden door.

Positioned on her side, Alaina noticed that she lay on a small wooden cot, her head resting upon a pillow. She lifted it while attempting to sit upright.

What? Why... why can't I move?

A muffled gasp escaped her as she quickly began checking herself. Her eyes widened as she suddenly realized that she was bound, her hands held behind her by several coils of rope tied tightly around her wrists. Glancing down, she found her feet to be restrained in a similar manner, securely tied together at the ankles. A strip of cloth covered her mouth, tied around her head to ensure that she remained quiet, as only muffled cries of panic could escape the gag.

Still somewhat weakened from whatever she had been drugged with, Alaina desperately writhed and squirmed against the ropes. A gasp leaked through her gag, her efforts to escape the ropes soon ending in exhaustion. She suddenly perked up at the sound of approaching footsteps. The metallic clank of a sliding deadbolt and the groan of rusty hinges echoed about the walls of her confines as the door creaked open.

The glow of the lantern upon the table revealed a young man as he entered. Black robes with violet trim flowed with his movements as he stopped before the cot. Long strands of jet-black hair hung over his shoulders to frame angular facial features as he stared down at his captive with a cruel grin.

"I see you're awake," he whispered, his voice serpent-like, as it carried a sinister lisp.

Alaina's gaze fell upon a slender length of ivory that was tucked into a leather belt around the young man's waist, its form in the likeness of a human femur. A large chunk of black obsidian rested in one end. Her eyes widened with instant recognition and fear.

The Rod of Veros!

Upon seeing the Rod, Alaina knew that it was Jerrod who now stood before her. A shudder coursed through her as all became clear. Jerrod must have somehow known that she and her companions were pursuing him. He had to be responsible for the thieves' attack on Divana. Pondering whatever means he had used to strike a bargain with them was irrelevant at this point. Alaina had far graver things to worry about, as she was now his prisoner.

Reaching down, Jerrod hooked his fingers in the gag. A gasp of air burst from Alaina as it was yanked down from over her mouth.

"Comfortable, my dear?" he hissed.

Shifting in discomfort against her restraints, Alaina frowned. "So you're Jerrod."

"Indeed," he replied while lowering himself to face-level with Alaina. "You have been searching for me, and so here I am."

Alaina glared defiantly into his dark, beady eyes while trying to hide her fear. She hoped that he wouldn't use magic on her or, worse, the dark power of the Rod.

Jerrod's mouth shaped into a sinister grin.

"Where are the rest of your companions?"

"Forget it, snake!" Alaina spat. "I'll tell you nothing!"

Jerrod's eyes narrowed as he rose once more. "Very well, then." He sneered. It matters not. They will come for you soon, I'm sure, and when they do, they will be destroyed."

"Why are you doing this?" Alaina frowned. "What has Veros promised you?"

Jerrod smiled.

"Power, my dear."

Alaina cringed as Jerrod leaned over her. She winced as the stench of his hot breath caressed her cheek and ear. "Power the likes of which you could never begin to comprehend... power I never could have gained from that old fool Agamemnon."

"You're the fool, Jerrod," Alaina retorted. "Whatever Veros has offered you is surely nothing but lies and deceit. He's only using you to get what he wants."

Jerrod only stared down at Alaina as she continued trying to convince him to do the right thing. "Don't do this, Jerrod. Come back with us and bring the Rod back to Agamemnon. I'm sure he'll..."

Alaina was suddenly interrupted, her attempts at reason reduced to muffled speech as Jerrod lifted the gag back into place over her mouth.

"Do forgive me for bringing our conversation to a close, my dear, but I have engagements to keep, and I cannot be delayed."

With that, Jerrod turned to leave; pausing before a cloaked and hooded figure that waited in the doorway of the cell.

"See to it that her friends are properly disposed of."

The hooded figure gave a nod of his head. "Of course."

The door to the cell was pulled shut with Jerrod's departure, the sharp clunk of the deadbolt on the door's opposite side causing Alaina to wince as it once more slid into place. Bound and helpless, she resumed her unavailing struggles alone in the silent darkness.

Halvar frowned as he stared down the trash strewn alley. "This is the place," Divana said, holding up a hooded lantern to light the area, as the arrival of night had now consumed all. The group moved quietly through the darkness, while scanning the area.

Divana turned away from the body of the thief that she had slain, who still lay as she had left him.

"Hey," Darrius suddenly called out while examining one wall. "Over here."

The group gathered around to see his find. "Blood," he said.

"Somewhat fresh, too," Grimm added.

"Alaina hurt one of them I think," Divana offered.

"Keep looking," Halvar instructed. "By the Powers of Light, I pray we are not too late."

Darrius and Grimm continued along the wall. Spotting a few more droplets and flecks of blood, they followed the trail to a hole in the base of the wall. Darrius turned to Halvar.

"Trail ends here."

Kneeling down, Halvar examined the hole. "Looks big enough to crawl through," he observed while peering inside. "It's too dark to see anything, though. I'm gonna check it out."

"Be careful," Divana warned as Halvar wormed his way through the opening, followed soon after by the others once his passage had seemed to go safely.

"C'mon, pull," Grimm grumbled as Darrius assisted him in fitting his stocky form through the opening.

"It looks like some sort of storage house," Divana stated while casting the lantern's light about. Wooden crates and barrels were stacked neatly about.

"Let's fan out..." Halvar suggested while lighting a lantern for himself.

Seconds passed as the group's investigation ensued.

"Hey, I found some more blood over here," Divana called out as she looked back from several stacks of crates that were grouped together at the back wall.

Darrius examined the crate as the others assembled around him. "That's odd..."

Reaching for the crate's top, he carefully lifted and removed the wooden lid, a smile forming as he peered inside. "Clever way to hide a secret passage," Halvar commented as all gathered to peer down the ladder that led down below the storage house. "Divana, you should go and bring the constable. I'm sure they'll want these thieves brought to justice, and besides, this may not be the safest place for you to be."

"We're not really sure what we are up against yet," Darrius added. "We may need all the help we can get."

Divana nodded before returning to crawl back through the hole to the outside. Hoisting himself over the edge of the crate, Halvar twisted to position himself. Grasping the crate's edge once inside, he placed his foot on the top rung of the ladder and began his descent. Darrius again assisted the burly Grimm in following Halvar's lead before he himself climbed down.

A musty smell in the corridor greeted the trio at the ladder's base, the light of Halvar's lantern providing the only visibility the cleric had as its glow flickered about the stone walls. At the hallway's end, a solid-looking wooden door came into view. Halvar frowned. Feint voices could be heard on the other side. Dimming the lantern, he drew his mace in preparation for a battle.

With bow and axe ready, Darrius and Grimm took the lead as all three crept along the wooden floor. Stopping before the door, the three listened to the voices on the other side, unsavory voices that hissed and planned ill deeds.

"And how do we know this Jerrod character is gonna give us what he promised?"

"He wouldn't lie to us."

"Yeah. He's our friend... completely worthy of our trust..."

Halvar frowned at Darrius and Grimm. "So Jerrod's behind this," he whispered. "He must have charmed some of these men with magic."

Darrius nodded in silent reply.

"So let's take 'em," Grimm whispered eagerly as the conversation continued in the room beyond.

"Agreed."

"So what should we do with the little warrior lady in the other room?"

"She's a little spitfire. Maybe we should keep her around... have a little fun with her..."

"Yeah... I like that in a woman..."

Laughter followed, filling the room. Halvar's ire rose at the thought of the thieves' plans.

Alaina!

In a flash, Halvar swung the mace with all his might. The wooden door splintered off its hinges from the blow's force, the cleric's rage surprising even Darrius and Grimm as he stormed into the room.

"Your villainy ends here, fiends!"

The five thieves sprang up from their seats at a round table in the room's center, a card game that had apparently been in progress coming to an abrupt end. Their hoods were pulled back to reveal weathered visages and tangled hair as their eyes flashed wide with shock.

"Well, I'll be damned!" Grimm bellowed, charging past Halvar. "The holy man's finally getting the hang of this!"

The thieves dove for safety as Grimm leaped at them. His axe demolished the wooden table as he swung the blade downward, the playing cards that once littered its surface scattered to the floor. Attempting to ready the weapon again, he snorted in disgust as he discovered it to be wedged firmly in a large portion of the tabletop.

"Son of a..."

Grimm's curse was interrupted as he suddenly felt a stabbing pain in his side. Glancing down, he spotted a small needle protruding from his flesh. Growling, he looked up to spot one of the thieves, a blowgun pressed to his mouth. He shook his head, a slight dizziness coming to him as he quickly yanked the projectile out. The thief's eyes widened in shock as Grimm braced a boot against the smashed table and yanked his axe free, seeming unfazed by the dart's toxin.

"You're dead meat," Grimm growled as he swung the axe fiercely. The thief evaded the assault with a plethora of acrobatic maneuvers as Grimm continued to press on with wild slashes.

From the doorway, Darrius fired an arrow past Halvar. The remainder of the thieves who were approaching Grimm from the rear dove and flipped to avoid the attack. One threw a dagger, the blade narrowly missing Darrius' shoulder as three others dashed in to engage him and Halvar.

The thieves lunged, the first proving too swift for Halvar to deflect his attack. The blade of the thief's short sword raked across the side of his neck. Halvar gasped, thankful to the Powers of Light that the chain coif had protected him as he blocked the attack of a second thief with his shield.

Halvar brought his mace around, dropping one of the rogues with a blow to the side as the other two broke off to attack Darrius, who dropped his bow and drew his own blade to parry a thrust. His cloak and hair flowed through the air as he quickly pivoted, dropping to cut across the back of his attacker's knee. The thief howled in pain as he fell, grabbing at his leg. Rising swiftly, Darrius slashed at the next thief, their blades clashing again and again.

With a determined glare, Halvar turned his gaze to the back of the room. Several chests and crates sat in one corner, presumably full of stolen goods. Directly across from him was a sturdy wooden door, a deadbolt slid into place to keep it securely locked. Above the roar of the battle, he could hear muffled cries calling out from behind it.

Alaina! She's in there!

He locked eyes with a lone thief who blocked his intended path, a dagger in his hand as he waited. Halvar pointed his mace at his foe.

"Powers of Light..." he started with conviction. "Hear thy servant's plea. Stop and hold thy enemy in the name of justice."

The thief rushed in, his attack suddenly halting mid-thrust as a nimbus of golden light surrounded Halvar's weapon. Surprise washed over him as he stood frozen in place, his body unresponsive as Halvar walked calmly around him.

Arriving at his intended destination, Halvar slid the deadbolt aside and shoved the door open. There before him, bound and gagged on a small cot, was Alaina. Her eyes widened with relief as he hurried to her side and pulled the gag from her mouth. "Are you alright?" he asked with concern.

"I'm alright," Alaina replied. "Jerrod was here... he's..."

"I know..." Halvar interrupted while working to untie her hands and feet. "We're getting you out of here."

Alaina couldn't restrain a brief smile at the thought of Halvar making her safety his main concern. Her smile soon faded as she turned her attention to the clashing of swords in the next room, the battle outside continuing to rage.

Back to back, Darrius and Grimm fought against the two remaining thieves. Time and again, Grimm's attacks cut only the air as the thief ducked, flipped, and dodged his attacks. "Quit dancin' around and fight like a man!" Grimm yelled.

Darrius' blade was knocked from his grasp as the other thief parried his attack. Twirling around, the cloaked man caught him across the side of his jaw with a back fist. Darrius staggered backward, falling to one knee as the thief charged in. Flipping the grip on his short sword to an underhand one, he clasped its hilt in both hands as he drove the point of the sword downward.

Darrius barely managed to get his hands up in time to catch the thief's wrists, the point of the blade held just inches from his face. Suddenly, a woman's voice rang out through the chamber; bold and commanding as two words came forth.

"Arrak Alabarr!"

A cry of agony erupted from the thief as he flew aside, causing Darrius to topple over, as well. The thief's sword clattered to the floor as he fell to lay in a fetal position, holding his side. Looking to where his aid had come from, Darrius spotted Divana in the entrance to the room, the hand from which the Mystic Bolt had come still extended. Four men shouldered past her, each clad in light leather armor and aiming a crossbow. "Nobody move!" one of them shouted.

The battle ceased as the last of the thieves dropped his sword, the others remaining still at the constabulary's order. Halvar emerged from Alaina's prison, her arm draped over his shoulder as he helped her along in her still somewhat weakened state.

Divana grinned. "Sorry I took so long."

Another man brushed past her as he entered the room, tall and regal-looking in a shiny chain shirt with a flowing red cape. His hand rested on the hilt of a long sword at his side as he looked about the room. "Well done, adventurers," he said before turning his attention to the band of rogues that lay about the floor. "And as for you thieves, it's off to the city dungeon with you."

Halvar and Alaina joined Darrius, Grimm, and Divana. All smiled as the thieves were placed under arrest.

Alaina stared solemnly out the window of her room at the inn. Korringlenn was quiet now, the full moon above casting its pale light over the streets and buildings of the city. Turning from the window, she made her way across the room toward the bed that would be hers for the night. Her pack, sword, and shield rested on the wooden floor at its foot. Walls of white were on all sides. Beyond the bed, a small hearth was located at the room's opposite side. A simple end table with a hooded lantern atop it sat next to the bed, as well. These features were the extent of the room's accommodations. It was a cheap room, no doubt, but it was a place for her and her companions to rest after their battle with the rogues, and that was good enough.

Seating herself upon the soft bed, Alaina sighed. All was well here in Korringlenn now, with the thieves who had been committing robberies in the city dungeon. Yet far greater threats were on the horizon, as the treacherous Jerrod had eluded them, still in possession of the Rod of Veros. The evil necromancer to whom the Rod belonged to was still out there somewhere, as well, waiting for his weapon to be delivered—a weapon which would no doubt unleash pure hell upon not only Korringlenn and the land of Adrinia, but all of Urith.

Lost in her thoughts, Alaina jerked up at a sudden rapping on her door.

"Who is it?" she called out.

"It's me," Halvar's voice responded from the other side.

Alaina grinned. "C'mon in."

Opening the door, Halvar stepped into the room, Divana following behind him to stop just at the threshold. Halvar cast a warm grin down at Alaina.

"How are you feeling?"

Alaina smiled up at him. "Still feeling a little weak, but much better..."

Divana sighed. "I'm sorry, Alaina. I feel like this was all my fault. If you hadn't come to help me, you wouldn't have..."

"It's not your fault," Alaina interrupted consolingly. "Jerrod set up that ambush."

"Indeed," Halvar added. "But Veros is the one truly to blame for all of this."

Alaina frowned. "I still say we should be looking for Jerrod rather than just sitting here doing nothing."

"You're in no shape to be fighting right now," Halvar replied. "You need time to recover your strength. Besides, we have no idea where to go from here. The constable said they would question those thieves tonight and let us know in the morning if they find any leads that will put us on Jerrod's trail. There's nothing we can do for now but wait."

Alaina sighed. She hated waiting, but deep down she knew that Halvar was right.

"We'll all meet downstairs in the morning and figure out what to do once we hear from the constable," Halvar said.

"I'm just glad you are ok," Divana chimed in. "Thank you for helping me. I wish I could be as brave as you."

Alaina smiled in spite of herself.

"Get some rest. We'll see you in the morning," Halvar said as he and Divana turned to leave.

"Halvar?" Alaina called.

The cleric's departure halted in the doorway as he turned back to her. "Yes, Alaina?"

Rising from her seat upon the bed, Alaina approached and stopped before him.

"What you did back there..." she started. "The way you came for me like that... was really brave."

"I..." He paused, casting his gaze briefly to the floor while he searched for the words. "I couldn't let them hurt you..."

Alaina grinned. "Thank you."

Lifting his gaze once more to her, Halvar produced a grin of his own while placing a hand upon her shoulder. "Good night, Alaina," he said before again turning to leave.

With soft eyes and a warm smile, Alaina watched him depart.

"Good night, Halvar Lightbringer."

CHAPTER
5
Lord of the Dead

I think I reached level three," Jake said.

"Yeah, me, too," Peter added. "I think we all did."

"I can't believe you rolled a one on that first attack," Josh said. "You even had the surprise attack bonus, along with the charge bonus on your roll."

"Hey, what do you guys want from me?" Jake asked.

"Is that why you always rush in like that?" Jennifer asked.

"He gets a plus-two bonus to his attack roll," Peter said, answering for Jake, who was engrossed in finishing off a can of soda. "I gotta take a leak, Kevin," he said as he crushed the empty can.

"Yeah, me, too," Peter added. Each tossed a glance at the other before springing from their seats in a race for the stairs, each trying to beat the other in the ascent to win first use of the bathroom.

"I think there's another batch of cookies up there and another twenty-four pack of cola," Kevin said before turning to his sister. "Help me bring 'em down, will ya, Jen?" With Jennifer in tow, Kevin made his way up to the kitchen.

Amy looked at Josh, who was finishing off the last of the cookies. Crumbs dotted the lap of his blue jeans and the front of the skinny youth's shirt. The short brown hair atop his head was slightly disheveled, hinting that he hadn't run a comb through it that day. Despite his unkempt appearance, he was a kind boy, never making fun of her in the way that Jake or Peter on occasion did.

Amy smiled. "You know..." she started. "The way you charged into the thieves' hideout to rescue me... that was kinda sweet."

Looking up, Josh grinned sheepishly. "Yeah, I'm a sucker for the damsel in distress, I guess..."

A twinge of embarrassment coursed through him. He could feel his cheeks flush as he lowered his eyes to the now-empty plate of cookies. He thought back to Jake's suggestion.

"Dude, I think she likes you... You should ask her out."

He had begun to think that maybe Jake was right. Maybe she really did like him. Amy continued to grin at him, and he wondered if the color of his face now rivaled that of a beet.

Josh and Amy were pulled from their thoughts at the sound of approaching footsteps, Kevin and Jennifer having returned with more soda and cookies. Jennifer set the new plate atop the old one in the coffee table's center and seated herself as Kevin worked his way past Josh to set the twenty-four pack of cola down and reclaim his seat at the table's head. More footsteps came as Jake and Peter returned and reclaimed their seats, as well.

"So who won the restroom race?" Kevin smirked.

"I did, of course," Peter gloated as all reached for the new plate of cookies.

"It's ok, I just went outside," Jake added. "Marked my territory like a wolf."

Amy shook her head. "So gross..."

"Anyway," Kevin said. "Let's get this ball rollin' again..."

Amy flashed Josh another grin as Kevin resumed the adventure.

"After a night of much-needed rest, you all meet up the next morning at a table in the Blazing Hearth Inn..."

"Ahhh...now that's good mead."

Grimm set the empty mug upon the table beside two others and wiped his mouth with the back of his hand. Alaina turned from the table to toss a glance past the inn's seated patrons to its entrance. "I hope the constabulary has a lead for us as to where Jerrod has gone," she said with a sigh.

Halvar reached past Divana as she quietly scanned over the pages of her spell book. "I have no doubt that the Powers of Light will show us the way," he said while claiming a warm muffin from a plate in the table's center.

Sipping at a goblet of his own, Darrius looked at Grimm, who waved his arms to get the attention of a nearby serving girl. "You drink more than a fish," He said, smirking as the serving girl placed another foamy mug before the dwarf. Grimm lifted the mug of mead with both hands and proceeded to gulp down the beverage, a small stream trickling from the corner of his mouth as the bottom of yet another mug slowly began to rise.

As Darrius lifted his own goblet once again, he spotted a man in leather armor enter the inn. With a hand resting on the hilt of a long sword at his side, he looked around the establishment for a moment before starting toward the group's table. "I hope that's the Powers of Light getting ready to show us the way, Halvar," Darrius said, nodding toward the approaching constable.

Alaina and Halvar turned as the constable stopped before their table.

"Well met, adventurers."

"Well met, constable." Alaina smiled. All in the group looked up at him, save Grimm, who continued to gulp his mead.

"What news do you bring?" Halvar inquired.

"Those thieves that we picked up all seemed to know that Jerrod fellow you're lookin' for. Apparently they accosted him shortly after his arrival, and when they did, he somehow convinced them to help. He claimed that he was being pursued and needed them to take care of any one askin' 'bout him."

Halvar frowned as their informant continued.

"They claim he waved his hands a lot and spoke funny. They're not really sure why, but most of them said helping him seemed like a good idea at the time."

"Sounds like a Charm spell," Divana offered.

"Well, they all said that this Jerrod character spoke of meeting someone important," the constable added. "In an abandoned silver mine in the hills, about half a day's ride north of here."

Alaina blanched. "Veros!"

"We must hurry," Halvar proclaimed as he tossed a few gold coins onto the table to pay for the group's food and drink.

"Let's ride," Alaina added as all sprang from the table, with the exception of Grimm, who hastily guzzled the remainder of his mead in a last-ditch effort to finish the drink before departing.

"Be careful if you plan on poking around up there," the constable warned. "I've heard tales of monsters in those mines."

"Thank you," Halvar offered to the constable as the group rushed past him.

"Good luck, adventurers," he replied as they hurried through the inn's exit.

With a deep sigh, Grimm set the spent mug upon the table and belched loudly. Grumbling, he hopped down from his seat and claimed his axe from where it leaned against the side of his chair. "Wait for me!"

The road leading to the mines had clearly not been traversed for many a year. The hooves of the group's mounts trampled the tall grass and weeds that had grown over the path as they galloped on. Arriving at the mouth of a cave, Halvar and Darrius dismounted, followed soon after by Alaina, Divana, and Grimm.

With a frown, Halvar peered into the darkness beyond the wooden frame and supports of the mine's entrance. A large wooden cart sat just inside, with a broken wheel causing it to lean slightly to one side. A pair of long wooden shafts protruded from within its interior, the handles of two picks that sat inside. The accumulation of rust indicated that the tools and cart had long since been forgotten. Alaina pulled a pair of torches from her pack. Lighting them both with flint and tinder, she handed one to Divana, keeping the other for herself.

Halvar turned to Darrius. "See anything?"

"The tunnel spans beyond my sight," Darrius replied.

"Well, what are we waitin' for?" Grimm grumbled as he readied his axe and shield. Brushing passed the others, he was first to enter the mine.

"Careful," Alaina warned as she and the others followed their bold companion. "The necromancer may be near."

"Not to mention the monsters that the constable warned about," Divana added while glancing around nervously.

With Grimm in the lead, Halvar, Alaina, and Darrius proceeded down the dark tunnel, followed closely by Divana. The light from the torches danced and flickered off of the walls of chipped rock, revealing an occasional abandoned mine cart and an old lantern that hung upon one wall. After traveling several yards, they came to a fork in the tunnel. Waving her torch, Alaina gazed down the left tunnel, then back again to the path ahead. "Which way should we go now?" she asked.

"We could flip a coin," Grimm whispered as he and Darrius stared down the tunnels.

"I hardly think we should leave our decision to chance," Alaina replied.

As the group quietly discussed what to do, Divana glanced uneasily to their rear. Without warning, a large, dark shape dropped from the ceiling a few feet from her. A scream of fright burst from her to echo throughout the tunnels, causing the others to turn and draw their weapons as the light of their torches revealed the form of an enormous arachnid.

"A giant spider." Halvar frowned.

The creature's body was nearly ten feet in diameter. Its eight long legs were thick and hairy, creating sharp clacking sounds upon the ground as it rushed forward.

Divana stumbled backward, falling to a seated position. The spider was upon her in a flash. With all the courage she could muster, she thrust out her torch in a desperate attempt to defend herself. The spider recoiled from the blaze and heat of the torch's fire, kept at bay for a brief moment as it scurried backward a few feet before raising its front and again rushing forward.

Halvar stepped in front of Divana, his shield raised for protection from the venom of the creature's large fangs as he readied his mace. Alaina and Grimm charged past him as Darrius drew and loosed an arrow, the shot finding its mark in the spider's exposed abdomen. Closing with the spider, Alaina swung her sword, hacking into one of its front legs. A second slash removed the extremity, causing the spider to clumsily skitter backward as Alaina held her torch up defensively. Raising his battle axe, Grimm leaped at the arachnid. A second arrow from Darrius' bow sailed past, burying itself nearly to its fletching as it pierced the creature's thorax. Bringing the axe down, Grimm managed to sever another of the spider's front limbs.

With a furious cry, Alaina again rushed in, thrusting her sword forward to punch the blade through the creature's left eye. Pulling the blade free, she and the others watched as the great spider writhed and convulsed, the curling up of its remaining legs and the stillness that followed a clear sign that their foe had been vanquished.

Alaina and Grimm returned their attention to Divana as she was assisted to her feet by Darrius. "Are you alright, Divana?" Alaina asked.

Divana pointed at the giant spider. "I'm fine, as long as we don't run into any more of those."

Grimm started down the left tunnel. "I guess we are going this way." Halvar said as he and the others cautiously followed.

"Sarcasm?" Darrius whispered in feigned surprise. "From a priest? I never knew you had it in you." Halvar only grinned in reply.

At the tunnel's end, the group entered a large chamber. More abandoned mine carts and tools sat in one corner. Long, silky strands were revealed along the walls, stretching across the room in some areas. On the floor in one corner was something cocooned in the strands, its shape vaguely humanoid in appearance. Swinging his axe, Grimm cut through some of the strands as he made his way across to investigate. Halvar and Darrius followed behind him as Alaina and Divana kept an eye on the area around and above them, having an idea of what may have been lurking in the dark somewhere beyond the torchlight.

Kneeling before the cocoon, Darrius drew his knife and sliced through the fibers. A dried skull peeked through the opening. Seeing that a dull mail coif loosely covered it, Darrius cut away more of the gluey strands to reveal a shriveled husk garbed in chain mail armor. Halvar noticed a golden medallion hanging around the corpse's neck, recognizing the holy symbol of a priest who followed the Powers of Light. Standing once more, Darrius placed a hand on Halvar's shoulder.

"He will have a decent burial when we return to town, my friend."

As the group prepared to depart, Divana was suddenly yanked off her feet. Her startled scream blasted the walls, causing all to turn as she was pulled straight up. "More spiders!" Grimm yelled as the group quickly traced the long, sticky strand from Divana's back to the large arachnid which hung from one itself directly above her.

Darrius drew and loosed two arrows. The first cut the webbing which held Divana, freeing her to fall feet first before she clumsily tumbled onto her back. The second struck the creature itself to send it crashing to the ground next to Alaina, who wasted no time in finishing the spider off as she brought the blade of her sword down between its large, round eyes.

Before Halvar, Grimm, or Darrius could move, a second and third spider dropped from the ceiling. One blocked their route, while the other landed behind Alaina.

"Behind you, Alaina!" Halvar shouted in warning.

The spider lashed out with one of its front legs as Alaina turned to face it. Her torch and sword flew from her grasp as she was sent staggering backward, her arms flailing as she suddenly collided with something soft and yielding. Trying to move, her eyes widened in horror as she realized that her arms and legs were trapped within the gluey fibers of the spider's webbing. In desperation she squirmed against the sticky strands, her strength insufficient to rip free as the spider began to scuttle toward its helpless prey.

Divana pushed herself to one knee, fearful as the spider quickly closed in on Alaina.

"Arrak Alabarr!" she shouted, flinging out her left arm. Three Mystic Bolts flew from her fingertips, striking the giant spider's back. Dark fluid poured from the creature's wounds as it spun to face the new threat. "Run, Divana!" Alaina shouted, still struggling to free herself.

Divana began to back away as the giant spider stalked forward. An arrow suddenly struck its side. The creature curled up, lifeless. Divana looked to see Darrius, his bow still aimed from the arrow he had just fired. Drawing her dagger, she moved to free Alaina as Halvar and Grimm engaged the remaining spider.

Grimm drove the spider back with several wild slashes before the creature lunged forward. Grimm raised his shield, the poisonous fangs slamming hard into it as he was sent toppling to the ground with the spider on top of him.

Halvar raised his mace.

"Powers of Light, grant your servant thy divine might..."

White flame engulfed the mace as he rushed forward. With a furious yell, Halvar swung the mace upward, the giant spider uprooted and sent flying from off Grimm to crash to the ground on its back. Picking himself up off the ground, Grimm watched as the dying spider's legs curled up. "I had him, ya know," he said to Halvar as they moved to join Divana and Alaina.

Halvar looked at Alaina as Divana finished cutting her free. "Are you alright?"

"I'm well," she replied before turning to Divana. "You saved my life... thank you..."

Divana grinned as Alaina placed a hand on her shoulder. "We should probably check out that other tunnel, right?"

Halvar nodded. "Yes, let's be off."

By torchlight, the group hurried back to continue their search down the other tunnel.

"Hey, over there!" Divana said, while pointing.

All in the group turned their gazes to the soft light of a lantern in the darkness beyond. By the yellowish glow, they could make out the silhouette of a robed figure several yards away. The figure quickly turned and fled to disappear from view, rounding a bend to the right further down the tunnel.

"Hurry!" Alaina cried as she and the others ran in pursuit.

"C'mon, Grimm!" Divana called back.

"I'm right behind ya!" Grimm called back, trying to hide his shortness of breath as he struggled to keep up with his longer-legged companions. "We dwarfs can move with great haste when we must..."

With Grimm bringing up the rear, the group sprinted several yards before rounding the bend, coming to a sudden halt as they entered a large chamber. Two more tunnels lay before them, as well as one to their left and one to their right. In the center of the area was Jerrod, another figure looming just over his right shoulder.

Standing nearly a foot taller than Jerrod, the dark figure was veiled beneath tattered black robes with crimson trim. A hood hid the being's visage, two pinpoints of intense red light all that could be seen as they shone from the darkness within. Jerrod grinned.

"Stand back, adventurers," he said with an air of confidence. "I'm protected by the might of Veros now."

All eyes in the party widened in horror as Veros' right arm slowly came into view. Extending from beneath the sleeve of his robe was his hand, its flesh now decaying and skeletal as its boney fingers firmly grasped the Rod.

Readying their weapons, the group watched as Veros' left hand crept eerily over Jerrod's right shoulder, coming slowly to rest there as the pinky finger touched down first, followed systematically by the other three. Slowly, Veros raised his head.

Light from the party's torches revealed a cadaverous face beneath the hood. Carrion- feasting worms writhed in his emaciated and rotting flesh, his empty eye sockets now only housing the two fiery dots of red light. Clearly, Veros was no longer among the living.

"Why, Jerrod?!" Divana demanded. "How could you do this?!"

Jerrod held his devilish grin, giving no reply as Veros spoke. The necromancer's voice was dry and crackling, like age-old parchment. "You have served me well, Jerrod," he hissed.

Suddenly, Jerrod's grin faded. His eyes widened as his breath suddenly caught in his lungs. His skin shriveled in mere seconds as the pallor of death came.

"Unfortunately," Veros whispered, "your usefulness to me has come to an end."

"No!" Divana cried out as Jerrod gasped for air. Within seconds, the youth started to decompose. Soon reduced to an aged skeleton before the group's very eyes, he crumbled to the ground, a mere pile of bones and dust. Veros threw back his head and released a desiccated laugh.

Darrius drew an arrow and fired. The group watched in shock and awe as the arrow struck Veros' chest, shattering on impact as though it had hit a wall of stone.

Halvar frowned. "He must be protected by magic!"

With weapons and shields ready, Alaina and Grimm charged. Before they could close with their foe, the undead wizard flung out his left arm, the fingers of his gnarled, rotting hand extended toward the heroes.

"Arrak Alabarr!"

A Mystic Bolt flew from each of Veros' fingertips. Sailing and swerving through the air toward their intended targets, each of the projectiles struck a single member of the group. Cries of pain erupted from each of them, their weapons and shields falling from their grasp as they were knocked to the ground. Another dry cackle crept out of Veros as he looked down at his foes, all of them lying in fetal positions as they held their sides in agony.

Clenching his teeth, Halvar fought through the pain, slowly struggling to his knees. Not yet ready to admit defeat, he lifted a defiant gaze to Veros. A thin trickle of blood ran from a corner of his mouth as he clasped the holy symbol around his neck.

"Powers of Light, guard thy servants in this dark hour."

With a stride of superiority, Veros stepped before Halvar. Seizing him by the throat with his left hand, Veros lifted him off his feet. Halvar's legs kicked as he was held from the ground with preternatural strength. He clutched the wrist of Veros' outstretched arm, wincing as his neck remained in the fiend's vice-like grip. Alaina slowly lifted her gaze, her eyes fearful as Halvar was held at Veros' mercy.

No....

"Foolish priest," Veros rasped. "You think that when you die, you go to your precious Powers of Light." Halvar's face contorted as Veros tightened his hold. "You come to me when you die..."

Turning toward the tunnel at his back, Veros flung Halvar across the chamber, his form crashing to the ground somewhere in the darkness beyond the passageway's entrance.

"Halvar!" Alaina cried out in desperation.

Slowly, Veros lifted the Rod above his head, the shard of obsidian at its end beginning to glow with an eerie black light. The ground began to churn and roil. Alaina blanched as several skeletal figures began to break through the dirt, many of them clutching picks in their boney hands as they dug themselves free of the earth.

Veros held up a decaying hand, a vaporous black mass rolling from the open palm. "Let those who lost their lives within these mines now claim yours," he hissed as his form vanished behind the cloud of inky blackness, with no trace of his presence to be found after its dissipation a moment later.

Alaina glanced at her remaining companions. While Darrius and Grimm had begun to stir, Divana remained curled up on the floor, barely showing signs of life.

A sense of panic began to wash over Alaina as she turned her gaze back to her undead foes, who numbered nearly a dozen. Fighting to ignore the pain in her side from the grievous wound, she forced herself to stand. Her legs quivered, barely able to hold her upright as she readied herself for battle. Grimm and Darrius slowly lifted their gazes, their eyes widening at the sight of the undead threat. The skeletons stalked forward as Alaina held up her sword and shield in preparation for the coming onslaught.

CHAPTER
6
The Quest Continues

O k," Jake started. "I'd just like to go on record and say that we are royally 'f'd' in the 'a' right now."

Jennifer looked over her character sheet. "I've only got one life point left."

"Yeah, I'm not doin' so hot on health, either," Peter added. "I think I'll try to get Divana to a safer place, since she's practically dead. Then I'll come back and try to help as best I can."

"Your arrows aren't gonna be as effective against these things," Jake said. "None of our weapons will be, with the exception of Halvar's mace," Amy stated. "Skeletons only take half damage from weapons that cut or pierce."

"Yeah, don't remind us," Josh said before turning to Kevin. "How far down the tunnel did Veros toss me?"

Kevin rolled some dice behind his screen.

"You went pretty far. You slid along the ground in the tunnel about ten feet from the point of impact, and the chamber is about twenty by twenty. Given the shape you're in, it'll probably take you a full combat turn to get back to the party."

"Well, if I'm goin' down, I'm goin' down fightin'," Amy retorted. "I charge at the skeletons."

"Don't worry," Josh said. "I'm gonna end this fight soon as I get there. I'm gonna use my repel undead ability."

Kevin nodded. "Alright, everyone roll for their initiative to see who acts first..."

With all the strength she could muster, Alaina gave an angry battle cry and rushed her undead foes. Breaking one to pieces by slamming into it with her shield, she ducked a pickaxe that was aimed at her head before coming back up to take out two more with forehand and backhand slashes of her sword. Raising her shield, she blocked another incoming blow before again lashing out with her blade. Block. Slash. Duck. Slash, slash.

Alaina battled valiantly, but her foes were many. Succumbing to her injury and fatigue, she lifted her shield one more time before the blow from the pickaxe knocked her onto her back. Another skeleton straddled her, lifting a pickaxe over its head. It was suddenly smashed to bits as a battle axe flew through the air to break through its left shoulder and collarbone.

Twisting her head, she spotted Grimm a few feet away, slumped to one knee after having hurled his weapon. "Get out of there, Alaina!" he called out as Darrius scooped Divana off the ground in a bridal carry, her body limp in his arms as he began taking her toward the relative safety of the chamber's exit.

Alaina rolled onto her stomach and pushed herself to one knee. With a backhand slash, she chopped through the knee of another skeleton to send it crumbling to the ground. Another approached her left flank, and she was barely able to block a horizontal swing with her shield. Alaina again crashed to the earth as the force of the blow sent her toppling over. As she lay on her side, her eyes widened as more skeletal figures emerged from the left and right tunnels. She and Grimm were surrounded. She hoped that Darrius had at least escaped with Divana.

Suddenly, a brilliant white light filled the chamber. The skeletons dropped their weapons and recoiled, shielding their faces and eyes as though blinded. Alaina turned to spot Halvar in the far tunnel. Clutching his side, he held out the chain with the holy symbol of the Powers of Light in his free hand. A look of determination shone in his eyes as the golden medallion shined with a brightness to nearly rival that of the sun.

"Powers of Light... return these mockeries of life to the grave from whence they came."

The skeletons began retreating, some re-interring themselves within the earth while others fled down the tunnels that they had previously come from. All was soon silent as the light quickly dimmed and faded. With the battle now over, Halvar took two steps forward before falling to his knees. Alaina crawled toward him, a look of concern etched on her face.

"I was afraid we had lost you," she said while pushing herself to her knees. Halvar smiled weakly. With a shaky hand, he hung the holy symbol back around his neck as Darrius returned to help Grimm to his feet. "Is Divana safe?" Alaina asked, she and Halvar slowly getting to their feet as Grimm trudged across the chamber to reclaim his axe.

"She is badly wounded," Darrius said solemnly.

"I will tend to our injuries as best I can once we get out of these mines," Halvar said.

Grimm leaned against his axe. "So now what do we do?"

"Maybe we should go find Agamemnon," Alaina suggested.

Halvar nodded. "Yes... he will know what to do."

"Veros is undead now?!" Jake said. "Are you kidding me?!"

Peter nodded in agreement. "He was damn near impossible to beat last time."

"And now he's even more powerful," Kevin proclaimed with a wry smile.

"I hope Agamemnon is more powerful, too," Josh said.

"Oh, he is," Kevin replied. "He hasn't done much other than study magic since you retired him. I actually added some more spells to his list, so he has some stuff that he didn't have when you were playing him."

"So we're just gonna get Agamemnon to take him out?" Jennifer asked.

"I doubt it's gonna be that easy," Josh replied.

Kevin grinned. "Oh, don't worry, your quest is far from over."

"Speaking of quests..." Jake interjected while holding up an empty soda box. "I think we're gonna have to go on a quest for more soda."

"I'm getting kinda hungry," Amy chimed in as she turned to Kevin. "I think it's time to put those pizzas your mom left for us in the oven."

"Sounds like a plan," Kevin said. "Anyway, your trip back to Illingrad is pretty uneventful. You camp during the two days back, I assume, rather than stay at an inn, since you wanna get back as quick as possible."

Amy nodded. "Right, we'll have to pass up the comforts of Korringlenn on the way back."

"Ok," Kevin said, standing. "We'll take a quick break, bake some frozen pizzas, and get some more soda."

"I can help," Jennifer offered while collecting the empty plate from the table that had held the cookies earlier.

"Jake and I can ride over to the gas station and grab some two liters of soda," Peter added. "They're open twenty-four hours."

All ran off to their chosen tasks, leaving Amy and Josh by themselves.

"I like your character," Amy said. "He's pretty cool. You usually play a wizard."

Josh grinned. "Yeah, I like magic users. Wanted to try something a little different this time, though."

"I've never played a cleric before, either," Amy said. "I like wizards, too, although thieves are my favorite."

"You seem to be having fun with the warrior," Josh observed.

Amy smiled. "Yeah, I guess I wanted to try something out of the ordinary, too."

The sound of approaching footsteps soon heralded Kevin's return.

"Pizza should be done in about forty-five minutes," he said while setting a glass of ice on the table before everyone's seat.

"Cool," Amy said as she began setting the alarm on her wrist watch. "Alarm will tell us when it's ready."

"Hey," Josh said. "That's smart thinking."

Amy only grinned in reply.

Kevin returned to his seat at the table's head. "Jennifer got a call from her friend, so she's on the phone with her at the moment."

"She really seems to like playing," Amy said. "You should have let her play a long time ago."

"Yeah," Kevin said, as though thinking back for a moment in hindsight. "Maybe I should have. Anyway, we'll just wait for everyone to get back and then we'll resume the adventure."

"Cool," Josh said. "Before we leave the mines, I'll heal everyone as best I can, and I'll recover that fallen priest's remains from the mines. Whatever belongings he has will be returned to the church. I'll pray to the Powers of Light for my spells that first night, since I used all of my healing spells on our wounds. Considering all that's happened, I probably won't be sleeping much that night."

"I more than likely won't be, either," Amy said with a grin. "Gives Alaina a chance to get to know Halvar a little better..." Josh turned to Kevin as he started to blush slightly. "I'm sure Jake wouldn't have Grimm argue, so he'd probably go ahead and sleep," Kevin said with a grin. "Darrius and Divana probably wouldn't object to a little more rest, either. I'll give you guys some bonus experience points for a little roleplaying while we wait for the others." Amy smiled as Kevin continued to rib Josh. "So with everyone else asleep, that leaves just the two of you..."

A full moon shone beyond the leaves of the trees overhead. The chirping of crickets and the croak of a tree frog resounded throughout the night as Halvar cast his gaze toward the sphere's pale glow. From the campfire at his back, Alaina approached to join him.

"Couldn't sleep either, huh?" she said.

Halvar produced a weak grin in reply.

"You should try to get some rest," she continued. "We still have another day's ride before we reach Grafton."

"I'll be alright," he said reassuringly.

Alaina placed a hand on his shoulder. "You're not alone in this. This burden is all of ours to bear, and we will fight at your side unto whatever end."

Halvar placed his hand upon hers. "Thank you... I am truly blessed by the Powers of Light to have allies such as you." She smiled as he continued. "Do not worry, I will rest soon. I'll wake Grimm or Darrius before turning in."

Alaina nodded, satisfied with his decision. "I will see you in the morning..."

Halvar nodded as she headed back to her tent to retire.

"Sleep well, Alaina," he said before turning his gaze back to the moon above. Lowering his head, Halvar clasped his hands together while slowly dropping to rest on one knee.

"Powers of Light... hear my prayers..."

"Got the sodas, dude," Jake proclaimed, holding up two two-liter bottles of cola as he and Peter came down the stairs, having returned from their trip to the gas station.

"We got some chips, too," Peter added while holding up two bags. "Bar-be-cue and sour cream."

"Cool," Kevin said before turning to Josh and Amy. "You two can have an extra fifty experience points for the roleplaying."

Peter and Jake reclaimed their seats and began pouring soda into the glasses of ice on the table as Jennifer came back down to the basement. "I'm back," she said, stating the obvious as she reclaimed her seat.

"Gee, really?" Kevin replied sarcastically.

Jennifer grinned. "I'm having a lot of fun, Kevin."

"Yeah, well, I'm... glad you are..." Kevin stammered, unsure of how to respond to the fact that for the first time, he and his sister were actually bonding.

Amy giggled as Kevin feigned a clearing of his throat.

"Alright, let's get this adventure goin' again, shall we?" he suggested, attempting not only to resume the game, but to change the subject to a less awkward one. "As I said, your two-day ride back to Illingrad is pretty uneventful, and you make it back without any problems. After returning the remains of the fallen cleric to the temple in Grafton for a proper burial, you meet back up with Agamemnon in his tower..."

A look of sadness formed on Agamemnon's face as he watched the group enter his chamber. "Veros has the Rod," Halvar said gravely.

"Jerrod is gone, as well," Divana added, her head lowering as the sadness of his demise crept into her heart.

"Then our time grows short, I fear," Agamemnon said. "With that rod, Veros can raise and command an undead army anywhere on Urith. He must be found."

"Veros has transformed himself somehow," Alaina said. "He, too, is now among the undead."

"The strength of twenty men he has now," Grimm added.

Agamemnon frowned. He stroked his long beard with one hand for a moment, as though in deep thought, before turning suddenly to rush toward one of the many bookcases along the walls. Mumbling to himself, he ran an index finger along a row of tomes.

"Let's see... necromancy..."

With that, he yanked a large black tome from one of the shelves and began thumbing through the crisp pages.

"You keep books on the dark arts?" Darrius asked with a hint of surprise.

"One should always know as much as possible about one's enemy," Agamemnon replied, his eyes shining as he suddenly ended his search within the leather-bound book. "Aha! Here we are..."

All gathered around the elderly wizard to see his findings. "He has transformed himself into a lich, no doubt."

"A lich?" Alaina asked.

Agamemnon ran an index finger along the text and symbols within the tome's pages. "Some who practice the dark arts transform themselves in such a manner in order to cheat death," Agamemnon explained. "The process is dangerous to the caster, but those who succeed gain the immortality and power of the undead by placing their life force within a specially prepared phylactery."

Divana's eyes widened in horror. "Immortality?!"

Agamemnon replaced the book in its original spot on the shelf and began gathering several other items. Books and scrolls with unknown contents, flasks with strange liquids in them, and a short, gnarled stick which had a power or ability known only to him were hastily tucked into a pack and into the folds of his robes before he began making his way down the spiral stairs to exit his tower.

"So how can we stop Veros now?" Halvar asked as he and the others followed.

Outside, Agamemnon began saddling a sleek black stallion for apparent departure. "There is but one way to slay him now," he said. "The phylactery containing his life force must be found and destroyed."

"How can we find it?" Alaina asked. "What's it look like?"

"The phylactery could be anything of immense value," Agamemnon said while mounting his steed. "I suspect that Veros would keep it nearby, however, to better watch and protect it." Musing, he paused for a moment before continuing. "To the east of here lies Black Marsh. Veros used to have a tower there. A vast crypt lies beneath it. My guess is that he would return to it to work his evil. I recommend you go there."

"Will you be going with us?" Divana asked, her eyes hopeful.

"I cannot," Agamemnon said. "I must ride west to the city of Adrinia. King Aldrich must know of the danger to come. I shall gather the dwarfs of Ironhelm and the elves of Sylverdale, as well, to further aid us. Veros' undead legions will no doubt come soon, and we must be prepared. You all must make this journey on your own."

Grimm and Darrius tossed a grin to one another, as they knew their fathers, the lords of their respective home cities, would no doubt be involved in the battle to come.

Reaching into the folds of his robes, Agamemnon withdrew a short and slender stick of gnarled wood. "Take this with you," he said, offering it to Divana. "Chant the words 'Lakkarr Ordellios' and this wand will negate magic within its vicinity."

With a nod of understanding, Divana took the wand. "The woods around Black Marsh will be too heavy to take a horse through," Agamemnon said. "You'll have to make the journey on foot."

Steering his horse by the reigns, Agamemnon turned it to face the west. Reaching into one of the saddle bags, he pulled a slender tube-shaped case from within, offering it to Halvar.

"This map should help you find your way," he said as Halvar took the case from his hand. "Make whatever preparations you must and be off. Find Veros and destroy his accursed rod. The fate of all Urith may be in your hands."

With a shout, Agamemnon spurred the stallion forward. In silence the group watched as he swiftly rode down the dirt street leading away from Illingrad and soon vanished in the distance.

"Ok," Kevin started. "Whatever provisions you think you'll need, you better get 'em now."

Amy began looking over her character sheet. "I'm gonna stop by the general store and pick up a hooded lantern, a few flasks of lamp oil, and some dry rations."

"Yeah, we wouldn't wanna starve to death." Peter chuckled. "We'll also get some extra wineskins there and fill 'em with water."

"And beer, too," Jake chimed in. Amy only disbelievingly shook her head in reply.

"You said that we'd have to make the trip to Black Marsh on foot," Amy said to Kevin. "We'll just leave our horses at the stables in Grafton and set out on foot from there."

"Fair enough," Kevin replied.

"I'm gonna stop at the temple to the Powers of Light," Josh declared. "I can pick up some holy water there. Could be useful against the undead."

"Yeah, it burns most of 'em like acid on contact," Amy added. "One d six points of damage, I think."

"Right," Josh said. "I'll say a quick prayer while I'm at the temple, too, before we head out. Then I'll meet up with everyone else outside the general store."

Kevin nodded. "Alright, you guys begin making your preparations..."

In silent prayer, Halvar knelt before the altar, his head lowered and his hands clasped before his chest. Opening his eyes, he raised his gaze to the large emblem of the sun on the wall above. Standing, he claimed his mace from atop the altar, along with a large metal helm that rested next to it and two flasks of holy water, a contribution from the temple that he had requested before departing on the dark journey ahead. Casting one more glance to the large idol of the Powers of Light, he placed the helmet over his chain coif and holstered the mace in his belt. Stuffing the flasks into a compartment in his pack, he claimed it and his shield before turning to leave.

Standing in the center of the aisle before him was a balding, elderly man. Clad in the white and gold robes of the priesthood, he held a sturdy-looking war hammer in his wrinkled hands. Halvar easily recognized him as the temple's High Priest. With a warm smile, he held the hammer out horizontally in both hands as Halvar stopped before him.

"Take this with you," he offered. "It will aid you in your quest, for it has been blessed by the Powers of Light."

Halvar recognized the hammer, for it was among the possessions of the fallen priest that he and the others had brought back to the temple from the mines near Korringlenn. Smiling, Halvar took the hammer in hand.

"Thank you, High Priest."

"May the Powers of Light watch over and protect you in your travels," the elderly priest said as Halvar continued up the aisle and through the temple's doors.

Divana stared at the building of brown brick. The wooden sign that hung from an outstretched pole above its door swung slightly from a gentle breeze, a depiction of a wooden barrel sitting within a coiled length of rope on it as the text above proclaimed the establishment to be Garrik's General Store.

Alaina, Darrius, and Grimm soon stepped out of the building and onto the dirt road to join her. "Get everything we'll need?" she asked.

"I think so," Alaina replied. "We should have enough rations and water to make the trip."

"I still say we were overcharged," Grimm complained.

Divana held up her spell book. "I took the time to prepare some spells that I think will help us in dealing with any magic that we should encounter in Veros' crypt."

All in the group suddenly turned as they noticed Halvar approaching to join them.

"That's quite a hammer you have there," Alaina said, observing the cleric's new weapon, which hung from his belt.

Halvar nodded. "A blessing from the Powers of Light," he replied while pulling out the two flasks of holy water from another pouch. "You should take these. They will help protect you."

"What is it?" Alaina asked, taking one of the glass containers while Darius claimed the other.

"Holy water... blessed by your temple's high priest, no doubt," Darrius stated.

Halvar nodded. "Indeed. Do we have everything we need?"

Divana took a deep breath, steeling herself for the dark times that she knew lay ahead. "We're ready when you are."

Halvar turned to face the east, his expression grave as he stared into the distance. "Then let's be off. Our quest continues..."

CHAPTER
7
Flight of Brom

Pizzas Ready" Amy said as the alarm on her watch sounded.

"I'll get it," Jennifer volunteered as she got up from her seat and headed up the stairs.

"So how powerful is that blessed war hammer that the High Priest gave me?" Josh asked.

"It does one d eight points of damage, with a plus-two bonus to all attack and damage rolls," Kevin replied. "Also, it'll harm things that are hurt only by magic."

Josh grinned while writing the statistics of his new weapon on his character sheet. "Sweet."

"I'm gonna help my sis with the pizza," Kevin said, standing. "Be right back."

Upstairs, Jennifer turned off the oven and removed the pizza with an oven mitt. Setting it atop the stove, she began cutting it into slices with a pizza cutter while Kevin took five plates and glasses from the cupboards above her, as well as a roll of paper towels from the counter.

"So you're having fun, huh?"

Jennifer paused for a moment from cutting the pizza. "Yeah, I am," she said with a smile.

Kevin grinned while watching her cut the pizza into ten slices for equal shares for everyone. "Well... I'm glad," he finally said.

Jennifer put the pizza cutter into the dishwasher before she followed Kevin back to the basement.

"Pizza is served," Kevin said while handing out plates and glasses. Each around the table took a plate with two slices as Peter filled a glass of soda for everyone. Squeezing past Amy, Jennifer and Kevin returned to their seats.

"I still can't believe Veros is a lich," Jake groaned.

"I ain't sweatin' it," Peter said. "I think we can take him."

"Alright, back to the adventure," Kevin started as he took a drink of soda and a bite of pizza, chewing as he continued to speak with his mouth full. "After passing through Grafton again, you guys begin making your way through the woods toward Black Marsh..."

The waters of the Krell River ran beneath the group as they strode along a large bridge of sturdy wood that stretched across it. From their position in the lead, Halvar and Alaina paused to stare ahead once they reached the bridge's end. The trees and foliage ahead had begun to thicken, the leaves of the large oak trees blocking much of the sun's rays. Divana cast a glance back toward Grafton, barely a mile back.

Alaina turned to Divana. "Homesick already?"

Divana sighed as Alaina placed a hand on her shoulder, taking a brief moment to offer her comfort and understanding before turning to continue the long journey.

Making their way amid the great tree trunks, Alaina and Grimm took the lead, cutting through any smaller vegetation that hindered their path with sword and axe. The group pressed on for many more miles in this fashion. Stops were brief, kept to brief minutes every few miles as the group replenished their tired bodies with a short rest, food, and water.

"My feet are killing me," Divana finally complained, after the group had traveled for most of the day.

Darrius looked to the sky, the sun starting to set in the path that lay behind the group. "It'll be dark soon," he said. "Another hour or so."

Halvar pulled out the map and scanned it for a moment.

"We still have many miles to go," Darrius said from over his shoulder.

Halvar nodded while placing it back in its case. "This will be as good a place as any to stop for the night," he said. "We'll make camp here and set out again at first light."

While Grimm moved about the nearby area to collect wood for a fire, Halvar and Darrius began unpacking to erect their tents. Breathing heavily, Divana seated herself upon the side of a large log that lay nearby.

Slipping the straps of her pack from her shoulders, Alaina laid it and her shield to rest on the ground. Taking a seat on the log as well, she turned to Divana with a playful grin. "Bet you sleep tonight."

Divana managed a tired smile of her own in reply. "I could sleep now."

Suddenly, all in the group looked up with a start as a loud roar blasted the stillness from somewhere in the distance. All activities instantly ceased as everyone's eyes widened with fear.

"What was that?!" Divana asked in alarm.

"Quick, hide!" Alaina said while grabbing her belongings. A second roar came, much louder than the first, as the creature responsible for the call seemed to be drawing closer. All in the group followed Alaina's example, dropping what they were doing to hide amid the forest's trees and underbrush.

Within moments, the roar sounded a third time, its volume at a near-deafening level as a great shadow fell upon the forest floor. There were several great whooshing sounds as the limbs of the trees overhead were flung to and fro as though blasted by fierce winds. From their hiding places, the

group held weapons close while casting worried eyes to the
sky above.

Overhead, a great beast soared. Stretching nearly four
hundred feet in length, the reptilian creature was covered in
dull red scales from head to tail. Four great limbs hung from
the leviathan's torso, each ending with sharp black claws. A
pair of leathery, bat-like wings stretched from its sides just
behind the shoulders, each as long as the beast itself as it
flapped them several times to remain aloft. Its long neck
stretched out as it turned its massive head to look around,
golden eyes with slitted pupils scanning the area from beneath
a pair of long black horns. Wearily, the group watched as the
huge beast flew on, its long tail stretching behind it as it
released another mighty roar.

"It's a red dragon," Divana whispered.

Grimm frowned. "It is best we not be seen," he said.

Darrius nodded in agreement. "Indeed... this would be an
adversary beyond any of us."

"Looks like it's headed north," Alaina said. "You think it's
Brom?"

"We'll wait for it to pass," Halvar suggested. Alaina
nodded in silent agreement.

Divana watched in awe as the mighty creature flew on.
Agamemnon had many volumes on the subject of dracology
in his library, and she had read much about them. Tales of the
red dragon were the stuff of legend and dread, great flame-
spewing leviathans who reduced entire villages to ash and
consumed the flesh of young maidens. The scales of a dragon
were said to be stronger than any shield, and she had heard
bards tell frightful stories of entire armies and adventuring
bands being decimated by teeth and claws that were sharper
than any man-made blade.

She had read of other species, as well, vile beasts of green
and black that roamed the forested hills and swamps,
respectively, as well as majestic creatures of gold, silver, and
copper that lived in mountainous regions and acted for the
cause of good.

Divana had never actually seen a dragon before until now. She surmised that this particular fiend was none other than Brom the Red, for which the range of mountains to the far north had been named. His claim of territory was vast, and she knew that for her and the others, being seen would make them all a potential meal. A chill ran down her spine at the mere thought of it.

A sigh of relief escaped all as the dragon soon disappeared into the horizon, its roar still echoing for a few more seconds in the distance.

"That was way too close for comfort," Alaina said as all emerged from their hiding places.

Halvar nodded. "Let's make camp and try to get a good night's sleep," he suggested. "We still have a long journey ahead of us."

CHAPTER
8
Black Marsh

T he leafy branches of the forest's oak trees were soon but a fond memory, replaced by duckweed and bulrushes. The earth beneath the group's feet had begun to soften as wet, squishy sounds were produced with each step onward. Patches of fog had begun to roll along the ground as the faint odor of stagnant water crept into the group's nostrils. Camp was set again in as dry a spot as the group could find before a third day of travel began.

Breaking camp, the group pressed on beneath a darkened sky. The buzz of insects surrounded them, one occasionally flying near a face or ear to prompt an agitated swat or wave of a hand. Damp, chill air caressed their skin. All in the party knew that they had entered Black Marsh.

Keeping close to Halvar and Alaina, Divana glanced around the dismal bog. Goosebumps rose as she recalled Agamemnon's stories of how the land had been transformed by Veros' dark sorcery to become the desolate swamp that it was now. She shivered at the thought of undead horrors or other monsters lurking in the muck and mire, waiting to drag the unwary down to their doom. "How much further do we have to go?" she asked nervously.

Halvar pulled out the map as Alaina held a hooded lantern over his shoulder for more light. "We'll hopefully reach the remains of Veros' Tower by nightfall."

"I don't see how you can tell night from day in this place," Grimm grumbled.

"Trust me, friend, you'll know," Darrius replied as Halvar replaced the map in its case.

Hours passed as the group continued, the quagmire's murky waters soon rising above their ankles. "These boots were suede," Divana complained with a sigh of exasperation.

"Well they're rawhide now," Grimm replied. "Might as well get over it." Divana only frowned in reply. "You know what I really hate about swamps, though?" Grimm continued as they trudged on.

"No, what?" Divana inquired.

Grimm pinched his nose shut with his index finger and thumb. "The damn smell," he replied gruffly. "It reminds me of..."

"Hold it," Alaina suddenly interrupted while holding up the lantern. The others stopped around her as they all spotted the scaly head and back of a large crocodile, the rest of its form hidden beneath the water's surface as it drifted across their intended path.

"Better wait for it to move on before we continue," Darrius suggested.

"The water over there looks like it might be deep," Grimm added.

Halvar nodded. "Agreed. Perhaps we can find a spot that's easier to traverse."

"Yeah, and hopefully drier," Divana chimed in.

The group continued to watch the crocodile as it coasted along the water's surface and climbed up onto an embankment before slowly scurrying on to disappear amid the vegetation.

"Over there," Darrius said, pointing at several more mounds that stretched along the intended path of the adventurers.

"Looks like that's our way across," Alaina said as she and Halvar began making their way along the drier path with Divana, Grimm, and Darrius at their backs.

A sudden bubbling of the water to the group's right grabbed everyone's attention, a gasp escaping Divana as she started. "What was that?"

Three more bursts churned the waters.

Alaina frowned. "Take the lantern, Divana."

Relinquishing the item, she brought her sword and shield to the ready. Halvar, Grimm, and Darrius followed her example as the water bubbled twice more. Darrius swiftly drew and loosed an arrow into the depths.

Grimm glanced briefly at Darrius. "A little jumpy, aren't we?" he said, with no reply given. Tension passed in the seconds to follow. There was only silence. "See?" Grimm continued. "Nothing to worry 'bout..."

Suddenly, the water before them erupted like a geyser, forcing those with shields to raise them to block the downpour while Darrius and Divana protected themselves as best they could with their arms. Large, frilled reptilian heads, five in number, broke the surface of the murky waters. Each rose nearly twenty feet above the party, held aloft by long necks of black leathery hide. The heads stared down at the group, amber eyes with slitted pupils darting about as each opened a large, toothy maw. A series of ear-splitting roars blasted the party's ears, causing them all to wince at the sound.

Darrius looked at Grimm. "You were saying?"

"What are they?!" Divana shrieked.

Halvar frowned. "I'm not so certain that this is more than a single creature."

Darrius swiftly loosed another arrow, his aim true at it buried itself deep into the left eye of one head. A loud shriek resounded as the head shook back and forth. With teeth bared, the head swooped down in response. Darrius dove to the side just in time to avoid the loud clack of colliding enamel that accompanied a savage bite.

Grimm moved quickly, swinging his axe down to cut deep into the exposed neck of the beast. Alaina joined the attack, as well, swinging her sword down with a fierce battle cry. The combined efforts of Grimm and Alaina's blades severed the head of the creature, the bloody stump rising into the air to flail about aimlessly.

Suddenly, a strange metamorphosis occurred. The headless neck began to split vertically down its center. Flesh shifted and molded like clay as the neck split evenly in two to form a second extremity. The group watched in horror as each stump grew a new head, the number of flesh-rendering jaws now increasing to six.

"By the Powers of Light!" Halvar gasped.

Alaina raised her shield, the force of the blow sending her staggering backward as teeth raked against the metal barrier that she held before her. More roars came, and all soon deduced the nature of what they faced. The heads that they fought belonged, not to many beasts, but a single creature that lurked beneath the bog's depths.

"It's a hydra!" Alaina cried.

"Oh, c'mon, Kevin!" Jake protested. "Not a hydra!"

Kevin grinned almost malevolently.

"Are these things tough to beat?" Jennifer asked.

"Yeah, they're pretty badass," Peter replied. "Got a feeling we may take a bit of a pounding on this one."

Peter scanned over the stats on his character sheet before turning to Kevin. "Hey, I have the Monster Lore skill," he said. "Do I know how to kill a hydra?"

Kevin rolled some dice. "You've heard that fire stops the creature from regrowing its severed heads," he declared.

"Great," Peter replied. "I'll relay that information to the rest of the group."

"We can pull through this," Josh said optimistically.

"I hope you guys got this all worked out," Amy said.

Josh only grinned in reply.

"We have to use fire!" Darrius shouted amid the roars of the beast. "Only open flame will prevent the creature from regrowing severed heads!"

Clenching her teeth, Alaina again raised her shield to fend off another set of toothy jaws. "How do you know this?"

From behind protection provided by Halvar and Grimm, Darrius launched another arrow as he continued. "My father spoke of such a beast before."

"How come my father never mentioned a damn hydra before?" Grimm complained through clenched teeth as a set of jaws clashed with his shield.

"No time to ponder that now," Halvar interjected while swinging his war hammer at a pair of incoming jaws. The blessed weapon connected with a mighty blow to the snout, causing the head to retreat from its attack. It shook back and forth for a moment as though fighting off a daze before unleashing an angry roar.

"Divana, get some torches lit for us... and fast!" Halvar instructed. "We'll keep this thing off you."

Setting the hooded lantern upon the ground, Divana hastily dropped her pack and began rummaging through it. Pulling out two torches and a tinderbox, she hoped that the dampness of the area wouldn't hinder her ability to light a fire. Seconds passed as she repeatedly struck the flint against the steel, a sense of desperation quickly descending upon her.

C'mon! Light!

Divana gasped as a few sparks finally set the end of the torch ablaze. The heat and warmth filled her with a sense of hope as she used the fire to easily light the second torch. "I got it!" she cried out in excitement.

Dropping his bow, Darrius seized the two torches. Wielding one in each hand, he moved to Alaina's side as she valiantly fended of a set of jaws. Thrusting his left hand out, he jabbed one torch against the beast's snout, the creature bellowing in pain as its hide burned. From behind her shield, Alaina raised her sword and brought it down on the hydra neck; the head severed as she sliced through the leathery flesh behind it.

"Now, Darrius!"

Moving swiftly, Darrius thrust the torch again, this time plunging the flame into the bloody end of the long neck. There was a sizzling sound as it fell to the ground, the wound sealing instantly as it was cauterized by the open flame. The snakelike extremity lay motionless, smoke rolling from the charred stump as the massive head remained inert just a few feet away, its eyes set as a long, meaty tongue snaked over the teeth of its slack jaws. No new heads grew to replace that which had fallen.

Alaina gave a quick nod of approval as Darrius offered her the other torch. Dropping her shield, she took it in her free hand before both moved to aid Halvar and Grimm in their continued efforts to fend off the hydra's fangs. Divana, in the meantime continued to watch from a safe distance.

Joining Halvar, Alaina sliced into another neck while the cleric blocked gnashing teeth with his shield. A second downward slash from her sword proved capable of the head's removal, and open flame was again hastily applied after the beheading. Darrius assisted Grimm in a similar manner, leaping in to burn a severed neck after three well-placed chops of the dwarf's axe.

"Grimm, watch out!" Alaina yelled as she spotted a pair of jaws closing in on the dwarf's unguarded rear. Grimm turned, raising his shield just in time to intercept the hydra's bite, its powerful jaws clamping onto the edge of his shield.

Before Grimm could swing his axe, the hydra lifted him high into the air. His arm was trapped in the shield's straps as he was fiercely swung from one side to the other before slipping loose. Launched several feet from the battle, Grimm crashed onto the moist earth, his form disappearing within the swamp's vegetation as concern for his well-being washed over the faces of his companions. The hydra roared again, its deafening bellow seeming to proclaim a victory as it dropped Grimm's shield. Undaunted, Alaina released a battle cry of her own, charging in to aid Darrius as another set of jaws descended upon him.

Swiftly drawing his knife, Darrius plunged the curved blade up into the roof of the mouth, the hydra hissing in pain as its attack halted. Alaina was upon the beast before it could withdraw. She hacked into its neck with two slashes of her sword to claim yet another of its heads, Darrius applying flame to the wound after the decapitation.

The two remaining heads of the hydra recoiled, each hissing loudly as they glared down at the group. Weaving and swaying, their eyes stared down, sizing up the group. "C'mon!" Alaina screamed, her challenge to the monster echoing throughout the swamp. At her side, Darrius and Halvar remained ready to continue the fight as Divana rushed off to check on Grimm. Releasing another series of loud hisses, the hydra slowly began to sink back into the murky waters. A final series of bubbles broke the surface once it had disappeared from sight. Then only silence remained.

"Looks like it's gone," Darrius stated.

Halvar frowned. "Let us hope so."

With the battle seemingly finished, Alaina, Halvar, and Darrius sheathed their weapons as Grimm and Divana emerged from behind the tall grasses nearby.

"Are you alright?" Darrius asked.

"Yeah, yeah, I'm fine," Grimm grumbled while holding his arm.

Halvar held his hands over Grimm's injury, a faint aura of white light surrounding them as he spoke.

"Powers of Light, tend to this warrior's wounds so that his quest for the good may continue."

Grimm began to flex and rotate his arm, a grin forming beneath his thick beard as the pain subsided.

"We should get going," Alaina suggested while handing Grimm's shield back to him. "That thing may decide to come back." Grimm nodded in somber agreement, and the group hurried on, leaving behind the severed heads of the hydra, which lay strewn about the marsh.

"Ok," Kevin started. "You guys each get five thousand experience for defeating the hydra."

Jennifer looked over her character sheet. "I think I gained a level."

"I think we all did," Amy said while adding the new total to her character sheet.

Jake turned to Kevin. "Did the hydra have any treasure?" he asked eagerly.

"Afraid not," Kevin replied. "You don't find anything lying around the area, and you have no idea where the thing's lair might be."

"Well, we definitely ain't gonna go looking for it," Amy said.

"Agreed," Josh added. "We keep going."

"Alright," Kevin said. "You guys continue on through the swamp. You spot some more of the area's wildlife, like snakes, crocodiles, or big lizards. Occasionally, you hear strange moans somewhere."

"Zombies?" Jennifer asked.

Amy nodded. "Sounds like it."

"You figure it could be zombies," Kevin said, continuing after rolling some dice. "You don't run into any, though, and you aren't attacked by anything else during you travels. By nightfall, you reach the Tower of Veros..."

CHAPTER
9
The Tower of Veros

The area had grown far darker with the coming of night. "Guess you were right, Darrius," Grimm grumbled as he cast his gaze to the black sky above. "You can tell when it's night here." Darrius only smirked in reply. Alaina, Halvar, and Divana couldn't see more than a few feet ahead of them as they waved torches and a hooded lantern about.

"Over there." Divana pointed as the group suddenly stepped into a small clearing. Looming before them several feet away was what looked to be the ruined remains of an old tower. "Is that..?" Divana asked, unable to finish.

"Yes," Alaina answered with a frown. "The Tower of Veros."

Decades of neglect had clearly reduced the structure to a mere shadow of its former glory. Damp mosses clung to the gray stonework all around it. Though once it had perhaps stretched high into the air, the tower had crumbled, and only its base remained; its upper levels were now long gone. The large wooden door, now rotting and decaying, hung cockeyed by rusty upper hinges at the arching entranceway.

With weapons drawn, the group cautiously approached the ominous-looking ruins.

"It doesn't look like anyone has been here for a long time," Divana observed while holding up her lantern.

Halvar frowned. "Looks can be deceiving."

Alaina moved forward, inspecting the rotted door. "We gotta clear this outta the way."

Drawing his battle axe, Grimm stepped forward. Easily demolishing the door with a single chop to the hinges, he grabbed hold of it and flung it aside to fall flat upon the ground. "Door's clear," he said.

Handing her torch to Halvar, Alaina readied her sword and shield. "So much for subtlety," she said while being the first to enter the ruins. Divana followed close behind her, holding up the lantern as Halvar, Grimm, and Darrius filed in as well.

Staying close together, the group crept through an aisle of broken and crumbling pillars, the light from Divana's lantern dancing off of the cracked stone columns.

"Sure is quiet," Grimm whispered.

Alaina frowned. "Yeah... too quiet..."

Halvar looked around. "Agamemnon mentioned a crypt beneath this place," he said in recollection.

"Hey," Darrius said, while suddenly pointing down the aisle of pillars toward the darkness beyond. "Over there."

Divana raised the lantern, its light revealing a large statue a few feet away. It was formed in the shape of a dragon, its wings wrapped around it as it sat on its haunches. A sphere of black iron was grasped in its front talons. It seemed to stare at the group as they approached it.

Sheathing her sword, Alaina stepped closer to examine the sphere. "You all thinking what I'm thinking?" she asked to the group as she grasped the sphere with both hands. Her face slightly contorting with strain, she grunted while hefting the sphere with only minor exertion. There was a loud click as the front limbs of the dragon rose slightly. The sound of grinding stone echoed throughout the chamber as the statue's base began to rise, revealing a doorway with a set of stone steps leading down. Alaina tossed the orb aside and redrew her sword.

"How'd you know to do that?" Grimm asked.

Alaina grinned. "Call it a hunch."

Halvar stepped forward to shine his torch into the darkness below. "Be careful," he warned as he followed

Alaina down the spiraling stairway, with Divana, Grimm, and Darrius guardedly trailing behind him. The slow descent seemed to last an eternity. The flickering light of flame peeked around the wall near the bottom of the steps, lit sconces along the smooth stone walls to their right greeting them as they stepped into a narrow corridor at the stairway's base. Peering ahead, the group spotted an arching doorway at the corridor's end. More firelight danced about from beyond the portal.

Alaina tossed a glance back to her companions, and Halvar gave a nod of reassurance before she continued to lead the others forward. All was silent, the sound of their footsteps all that could be heard as they echoed off the walls.

Halfway down the corridor, all halted their advance as they noticed strange symbols etched into the wall to their left. "Whadaya make of this?" Grimm asked.

Darrius studied the wall for a moment. "Looks like another secret passage," he replied. He ran his hands along the wall for a few moments. "I can't seem to find a way to open it."

Alaina scanned over the symbols. "Maybe these have something to do with opening it," she said before turning to Halvar. "Can you read it?"

Halvar shook his head. "I'm afraid it's in no language that I am familiar with."

Divana stepped forward and placed her hand upon the wall. "Alagor. Beladramor..." she whispered while briefly closing her eyes in concentration. After a moment, she removed her hand from the wall. "The writing is magical," she said.

"How you know that?" Grimm asked while resting his axe on his shoulder.

"She's a wizard," Alaina said in a sarcastic tone. "If anyone would know about magic, I'd think it would be her."

"I cast a spell that detects magical auras," Divana answered.

"Can you read what it says?" Darrius asked.

Divana mused momentarily. "No, but I know a spell that might enable me to translate it..."

"I've got the Read Magical Text and Translate Language spells," Jennifer stated.

"That should get the job done," Josh said.

Amy nodded in agreement. "You said the writing was magical," she said to Kevin before again addressing Jennifer. "Try casting Read Magical Text."

Jennifer turned to Kevin. "I'll cast that," she declared.

"Alright," Kevin replied. "As you prepare to cast your spell..."

Suddenly, all looked down the corridor in alarm as a low moan resounded from the arched doorway at its end. Several human figures stumbled into view. The light of the corridor's torches revealed tattered loincloths and rotting flesh, the dead eyes of the walking corpses locked on the group as they ambled forward with arms slowly rising to outstretch.

"Zombies!" Divana cried.

"I really hate these things," Grimm said before releasing a bellow of rage and charging down the corridor. Darrius swiftly drew and fired an arrow, dropping the first of the zombies to enter the hallway as the arrow found its new home between the creature's eyes.

"C'mon," Alaina said. "I got a feeling that he's gonna need help."

Halvar turned to Divana as Alaina and Darrius rushed after Grimm. "See if you can get this passageway opened. We'll try to keep these things off you."

Divana nodded as the cleric pulled the holy symbol from around his neck. "May the Powers of Light protect you," he said before dashing off to join the others.

Divana turned her attention back to the wall. "Ok, let's see here…" she said thoughtfully, beginning her examination the arcane symbols as the battle down the hall raged.

Grimm leaped over the fallen zombie in the doorway, crashing into another with his shield to send it staggering backward as he plowed his way through the portal. Brandishing his battle axe like a crazed madman, he waded into the undead horde, severing limbs and heads with wild slashes as Alaina, Darrius, and Halvar soon joined his side.

All in the group recognized the large, circular chamber that they had now entered. Two large pits of flame burned in the room's center, and a flight of stairs at the back of the room which led to a throne of bones. This was the chamber where Agamemnon and his allies had their last battle with Veros.

Alaina swung her sword downward, chopping down one zombie as she sliced through its collarbone and shoulder. An arrow from Darrius' bow sailed past her to drop another as she severed the head of a third with a backhand slash. Pressing on with continued attacks, Alaina managed to put her back to Grimm's.

Swinging his ax, the dwarf severed the leg of another zombie, the creature clumsily falling onto its back. "You know what I hate about zombies?" he shouted as he brought his axe down on the head his prone foe.

Alaina held up her shield to fend off another trio of corpses that clawed at her, the creatures grabbing hold of its edges in an attempt to pull it aside and get to her. "The smell, right?" she shouted back to Grimm in reply while slashing the throat of a fourth zombie at her flank.

"Have I mentioned it before?" Grimm asked while hacking and slashing wildly.

Holding out his holy symbol, Halvar stepped forward. The golden emblem glowed brilliantly in his hand, earning Alaina and Grimm a brief reprieve as many of the creatures recoiled in fear. More continued to advance, however, the very evil of the place seeming to work against the divine power which Halvar channeled through him.

"There's too many of them!" he called out as Darrius rapidly volleyed more arrows at the zombies. "I can't repel them all!"

"I'm getting a sense of déjà vu here," Amy said.

Josh nodded. "Yeah, tell me 'bout it."

"Bad news, guys," Peter started while looking over his character sheet. "I've only got nine arrows left."

"Well, isn't that delightful," Jake said sarcastically. "I'm just gonna keep choppin' up zombie ass. That's been workin' pretty good for me."

"So what does that strange writing on the wall say?" Jennifer asked, shifting the attention from the rest of the group's plight to her own. "I'm casting Translate Languages."

"Well, while you all are fighting for your lives..." Kevin said before turning to Jennifer.

Divana waved a hand before the wall. "Aladaross... Sarra... Bennadross..." Closing her eyes, she then placed her hand against it once more and began to chant. "Haladuall... Durall... Haval Quinn Clovisquill... Noctural Sanguinn... Phallickill!"

The grating of stone echoed throughout the walls of the crypt. A startled gasp burst from Divana as she jumped back. "Yes!" she cried in excitement as the wall slowly slid aside.

Another corridor, much like the one in which she stood stretched out before her. Tossing one more glance toward the sounds of her allies' battle with the zombies, she held up her lantern and stared into the dark. "Looks like it's up to me," she whispered to herself, as her allies were no longer in view.

With much reluctance, Divana began making her way into the darkness of the new passageway. The hall seemed to go on forever as she cautiously pressed on, her lantern providing the only light within the narrow space. A chill ran down her spine, her blood running cold as she paused to ponder what horrors possibly awaited her.

Be brave, Divana...

Mustering the courage to continue on, she finally came to a wooden door at the corridor's end. Taking a deep breath, she steeled herself for whatever might lie behind it before she extended a trembling hand. Grasping its brass handle, she pulled at it. The door wouldn't budge. Scanning the door, she saw no locking mechanism.

Must be magically sealed... Oh, of course!

Remembering the wand that Agamemnon had given her before she left, she pulled it from her belt and pointed it toward the door. "Now, let's see..." she thought aloud. "What were those words again? Ah, yes! Lakkarr Ordellios!" The slender stick of gnarled wood glowed faintly in her hands, the wooden door before her shimmering slightly soon after.

Hope that did the trick...

Tucking the Wand of Magic Negation back into her belt, Divana pulled on the door's handle again. Its rusty hinges responded with eerie creaks and groans as it opened into a large chamber. Peering inside, she gasped in fright as the light of her lantern revealed a macabre sight.

Divana gagged as the stench of decay assailed her. Scanning the area, she blanched upon seeing several stone slabs that were lined up at the room's left side. Leather straps and metal buckles dangled unfastened from their sides, the surface of all stained with old blood and grime. Two long wooden tables sat on the room's right side. An assortment of surgical tools littered the surface of the first, the blades of the assorted scalpels and saws all caked with gore. Beakers and tube racks of varying sizes and shapes adorned the surface of the second, along with an hour glass and a distiller.

Looks like a laboratory of some sort...

Divana suddenly caught a shuffling sound in the darkness. A cry of fright burst from her as she suddenly spotted two ambling corpses that slowly made their way toward her amid the stone slabs. Her eyes widened in fear as she took a few steps back from the shambling creatures. Mustering as much courage as she could, Divana flung out her arm while pointing her index finger at the zombies.

"Arrak Alabarr!"

Three Mystic Bolts flew from her finger, two striking unerringly to drop one of the rotting horrors as the third struck the other. Divana blanched as the zombie continued its clumsy gait, its arms outstretched as it reached for her. In desperation, Divana dashed away, narrowly avoiding clawed fingers that grabbed for her as she moved to keep one of the stone slabs between her and her undead attacker.

With another fearful cry, Divana flung the lantern at the zombie as it continued to reach for her, the abomination seeming to lack the intelligence to climb over the slab to get at her. The lantern broke apart as it smashed into the creature's chest, a low moan emanating from it as its torso burst into flames almost instantly. Backing into another of the slabs at her rear, Divana watched as the creature fell to the ground, motionless.

Setting her pack upon the floor, she began rummaging through it to extract a torch from amid its contents. A look of revulsion twisted her face as she moved toward the burning zombie on the floor, lighting her torch off the fire a few moments before the oil that fueled it burned out.

Waving the torch, Divana looked around.

Hope there aren't any more of those things...

Cautiously, she moved through the veritable chamber of death for further investigations. Holding up the torch, she suddenly looked up to notice another doorway across the room; the odd portal positioned about halfway up the wall.

That's strange...

Divana moved closer to investigate the peculiar opening. Stopping beneath it, she reached up toward its base; the opening taunting her, as it was several feet out of reach. Her eyebrows sloped into a furrow. She wished that Grimm were around, for she knew of the dwarf's ability to traverse mountains and scale sheer rock walls with the use of picks, ropes, and spikes, a talent which no doubt would grant easy access to the room. Frustration shined in her eyes as she made her way back to the room's opposite side.

There has to be something important up there...

Divana continued to stare into the opening. Straining to see whatever might be inside, she suddenly perked as the torch's light reflected off of something large and shiny. Surmising the object of her curiosity to be in the center of the elevated room, she pondered how to reach it, her eyes lighting up as an idea soon sprang to mind.

I know, I'll cast Invisible Servant!

Divana lay the torch down on the foot of one of the stone slabs, knowing that she would need both hands free to cast the spell. Extending her arms forward, she systematically wiggled the fingers of her left hand while pointing at the floor before her with the index finger of her right. "Alleron... Quevosmorda," she quietly chanted. A shimmering mass appeared briefly before her, soon after fading from sight.

"Ok," Divana quietly started, taking a moment to smile at her handiwork while pondering the proper wording for her request to the servant.

"Invisible Servant, bring to me the shiny object in the center of the elevated room that lies before me." She waited, the object soon coming into the torch's light as it floated down from within the opening to her awaiting hands. She gasped in surprise as her eyes finally came to rest upon a nearly life-size human skull, which had been finely crafted from pure diamond . Strange glyphs and runes had been etched into its top. Surmising the markings to be arcane in nature, her eyes widened as she deduced exactly what it was that she held.

This must be Veros' phylactery!

Divana started as she heard a raspy laugh. Dropping the golden skull, her eyes widened in horror as she spun around to see the lich standing in the laboratory's entrance. "Foolish girl," Veros hissed. "You have made a grave mistake in coming here."

Divana fumbled for the Wand of Magic Negation. With frightening celerity, Veros was upon her as she pulled the wand from her belt. Seizing her by the throat with his right hand, he grabbed her wrist with his left. With a vice-like grip, he began to squeeze Divana's arm, her grip on the wand soon relinquished as it fell to the floor with a clatter.

"I could pull the life out of you right now," Veros gloated.

Divana winced as the grip of the putrid hand on her throat tightened. She felt her feet leave the floor as she was slowly lifted up with a single outstretched arm.

"Or I could crush you with my bare hands..."

Clutching at Vero's wrist, Divana began kicking her legs as the lich suddenly began carrying her toward the stone slabs in the room by her throat. With tremendous force, he slammed her down on one of them, the force knocking the wind out of her as she crashed onto her back. Unable to move, she lay helpless as Veros began pulling the leather straps across her, cinching and buckling them tightly across her arms and torso. Moving toward the foot of the slab, he restrained her legs in a similar manner as he pulled two more straps across them to cross above the knees and over her ankles.

"I think perhaps I shall keep you around as a pet instead," Veros rasped while staring down at his captive. "You will make a fine servant in death, I am sure. Perhaps I can use you to deliver a message to Agamemnon..."

Divana squirmed against the straps as Veros continued.

"I will be back for you momentarily, just as soon as I have destroyed your friends..."

Divana's eyes shined with terror as Veros turned away. "No!"

The lich cackled dryly at Divana's desperate cry, his form disappearing from sight as he exited the lab. The flickering light of the torch's fire danced across Divana's prone form.

Alone in the dark, she writhed and struggled, her restraints seemingly inescapable.

"There's no way for me to break loose?" Jennifer asked.

Kevin shook his head. "Afraid not," he said while scanning over a chart in his Majik Master's Tome. "You only have an eight in your Might attribute. It's not high enough to break the straps."

"Damn it, Kevin," Jake protested. "We need her, not to mention Veros' phylactery that she found."

"Hey, it isn't my fault you guys chose to split up," Kevin protested while holding up his hands in defense.

"We gotta have that skull," Josh interjected. "It's the only way to destroy Veros."

Leaning toward Jennifer, Amy cupped a hand around her ear while whispering into it. Jennifer's eyes lit up as she quickly looked at Kevin.

"We can't keep this up forever!" Alaina yelled as she slashed at the seemingly unending horde of walking cadavers.

Grimm released a thunderous roar, his axe hacking into more of the creatures as arrows pierced the skulls of two before him. Glancing to his left, he spotted Darrius drawing another arrow. "C'mon!" Grimm yelled to Alaina before he charged through the mob that had surrounded them both. With a few more slashes of her sword, Alaina covered their retreat before turning into a full sprint as she and Grimm dashed towards Halvar.

Seven... Six... Five...

Quietly, Darrius counted his arrows, knowing that he had to make each one count. Three more shots found their marks, each sticking into the head of a single zombie to lend Grimm and Alaina more time. Reaching again for the quiver at his back, he turned to Halvar, who continued his attempts to repel more of the lifeless abominations.

Darrius' aim was again true as he volleyed another trio.

Four... Three... Two...

Reaching for his last arrow, his eyes widened as he spotted a gruesome sight. A hulking figure advanced amid the other walking corpses. Standing nearly eight feet tall, its range of motion was far different from the others. Its stride lacked their clumsiness, and its movements more resembled that of a living human being. Lines of stitches adorned its limbs, torso, and head; body parts and extremities appearing mismatched as they seemed to have been taken from corpses at varying stages of decay and assembled together to create the entity. While the pallor and stench of death still clung to the patchwork creature, a spark of intelligence and malice seemed to shine in its eyes.

Darrius blanched.

A flesh golem!

The thing stalked toward Halvar's rear. Darrius shouted a warning as it raised a meaty right hand to draw back a menacing fist.

"Halvar! Behind you!"

Turning swiftly, Halvar raised his shield just in time to intercept the incoming blow, his arm groaning in agony as the fist slammed into the protective barrier. His teeth clenched as he was knocked onto his back by the sheer force of the blow, the glowing holy symbol flying from the grasp of his right hand to skitter across the stone floor.

Alaina's eyes widened at the sight.

"Halvar!"

Breaking into a full sprint, she charged past several zombies with her shield -knocking them aside in attempt to reach Halvar's side as Grimm hacked and slashed his way through the undead mob with his axe.

Standing over Halvar, the golem raised both fists above its head in preparation for an axe handle blow. An arrow suddenly struck the creature's exposed ribs as Darrius fired his last. Staggering backward, the golem roared in pain and rage as a prone Halvar rolled out of harm's way. Drawing his knife,

Darrius rushed to join Grimm's side as Alaina closed with the golem.

Alaina leaped at the monstrosity with a furious cry. Thrusting her sword forward, she plunged its blade deep into the creature's chest. A black, viscous fluid oozed from the wound, the golem bellowing as Alaina yanked the sword back. The creature slumped to one knee as she again swung the blade, bringing it across to sever the golem's neck. The head dropped away as the creature fell forward with a sick thud at her feet.

Alaina turned to check her allies. Darrius and Grimm now fought together, each protecting the rear of the other as their blades brought down several zombies that had surrounded them. Before she could turn her attention to Halvar, a dark robed figure stride through the chamber's entrance.

Veros!

Alaina watched aghast as the lich produced the Rod from beneath the folds of his tattered robes. The shard of obsidian at its end glowed with a dark light as Veros pointed it forward. The bodies of the previously vanquished undead jerked and twitched. Slowly, the corpses began to rise to their feet as they animated to join the battle once again.

No!

Alaina dashed toward Veros. Using her shield, she bashed aside a pair of corpses to her left while using her sword to cut down a third that blocked her path.

*I've got to get The Rod away from him...*Charging on, she leaped at the lich with a back hand slash, knocking The Rod from his grasp to send it sliding across the floor of the chamber several feet away. Thrusting the sword forward, she punched it through Veros' abdomen, nearly burying the blade to the hilt as it exited out his back. Alaina's eyes widened in horror as no blood came from the wound. Veros' only laughed dryly, seemingly unharmed by an attack that would have killed any mere mortal. "Fool..." he hissed, before he landed a powerful back hand to Alaina's jaw. Spun and staggered from the blow's impact, Alaina's grasp on her sword and shield were relinquished as she dropped to one knee. Grabbing hold of the sword in his rotting hands, Veros casually pulled the blade from his stomach and cast the weapon aside before stalking toward Alaina.

Slowly pushing himself to his feet, Halvar gasped as he saw Grimm and Darrius fighting for their lives. Still standing back to back, their forms were soon lost amid the mob of walking corpses as they continued to hack and slash. Peering through the zombies that had gathered around him, he spotted a fallen Alaina a few yards away. His eyes wide with horror, he watched as Veros stopped at her side and seized her by the throat with a single putrid hand. Her face contorted in pain as he lifted her effortlessly into the air with a single outstretched arm. Clutching at Veros' wrist with both hands, Alaina's legs kicked as she writhed helplessly in the vice like grip. "You will pay for that with your life..." Veros rasped.

Halvar screamed in desperation as several zombies clawed at his shoulders, neck, and arms, threatening to drag him down.

"Alaina! No!"

Shoving some of the zombies back with his shield, Halvar managed to pull the war hammer from his belt.

Powers of Light, grant me strength in this darkest hour!

Tearing his arm free of a zombie's grip, Halvar began unleashing a series of forehand and back hand swings. Bones were shattered as bodies flew aside from each blow, the blessed weapon sending many of the zombies to slam into nearby walls with sick wet thuds. Halvar pressed on with his attack, a path soon cleared as he pushed through more of the creatures with his shield before charging straight for Veros.

Still in the lich's grasp, Alaina winced as his grip on her throat tightened.

I've got to free myself!

Her strength quickly fading, she fumbled for a belt pouch at her side, her right hand trembling as she extracted the flask of holy water that was tucked into it. Still gripping the wrist of Veros' outstretched arm with her left hand, she raised the flask above her head. With the last of her strength, she smashed it atop Vero's arm. The lich howled in pain as the broken container's contents washed over his putrid flesh, the blessed water burning and sizzling as though it were acid.

Alaina fell from Veros' grasp, landing upon her rump as the lich quickly recoiled. Favoring her throat but for a brief moment, she began to crab crawl backwards before spotting Halvar. Closing in fast, the priest's eyes shined with a righteous fury. White flames surrounded the hammer as he drew it back in preparation for a strike.

"Powers of Light, vanquish this evil!"

With all his might, Halvar swung the hammer; the force of the blow launching Veros across the chamber. Halvar was forced to pivot with the momentum of his attack as Veros crashed into a far wall of the chamber; the stonework cracking and breaking from the impact of the lich's body. Veros fell to the floor, chunks of debris covering him. Halvar turned to Alaina.

"Are you alright?"

"I'll be ok." she replied as she was helped her to her feet.

Halvar turned again to face the spot Veros had fell; chunks of the rubble beginning to shift and move as the lich began to climb out. "Go," Halvar instructed. "Help them and destroy The Rod. I'll buy you as much time as I can."

Alaina's eyes widened fearfully as she realized Halvar's intent to do battle with Veros one on one.

"But you can't..."

"I said go!" Halvar urgently interrupted. His gaze remained on Veros as the lich emerged from the debris. Stepping out of the cloud of dust, his gaze piercing and hate filled as he and the Halvar began to engage in a stare down.

With reluctance etched in her face, Alaina dashed off. Reclaiming her sword and shield which lay but a few feet away, she tossed one final glance toward Halvar before taking off. Several feet ahead, she saw Grimm and Darrius continuing their struggle. Their cries of battle rose from within the mob as their forms were lost amid the hoard of walking corpses what threatened to drag them down.

Swinging her sword with renewed vigor, Alaina waded into a veritable sea of rotting flesh as Grimm and Darrius' struggles had reached an end; the hands of the undead masses clawing and pummeling them to the ground. "Darrius!" Alaina shouted while continuing to fight. "Use the holy water!"

With the last of his strength, Darrius tore his right arm free of one zombie to thrust the blade into the head of another that gripped his left. Pulling the flask of holy water from his belt, he popped the stopper off with his thumb and swung his arm outward. A stream of the liquid trailed before him, the creatures withdrawing with low moans as their putrid flesh burned. Darrius turned and splashed more of the blessed water on Grimm's foes. The dwarf erupted from the grasp of his attackers, flinging those zombies that were untouched by the water off of him. With a roar he resumed his attack, slashing wildly with his axe at the zombies as he and Darrius were joined by Alaina. "We've got to destroy The Rod!" she cried while fighting alongside Darrius. "It's our only chance!"

Darrius spun and threw the flask at the zombies to his back, lending Grimm more aid as he hacked and slashed at the retreating zombies. "Go!" Darrius instructed to Alaina. "We'll hold them off!"

Raising her shield, Alaina again charged. Several zombies were knocked down or aside as she rammed into them. Following behind her, Darrius knifed any that fell as Grimm in turn moved to protect his rear. A few more well placed slashes put Alaina in position as she locked determined eyes on her target, The Rod of Veros laying just a few yards away.

It's no use... I can't break free!

A gasp of exhaustion burst from Divana, panic consuming her in her failing efforts to escape the leather straps. Her eyes were wide with fear as she glanced about the chamber. The light from the torch that lay on the slab next to her had begun to flicker and dim. She knew it would soon burn out, leaving her in total darkness.

Seconds passed as Divana continued to wiggle and squirm against the restraints. Suddenly, she gasped in startled recollection.

Of course! The Invisible Servant... I can use it to get free!

She remembered casting the spell to fetch Veros' phylactery, and knew that the arcane energies that produced the servant lasted for an hour before expiring. Lifting her head, she stared beyond the foot of her slab; taking a moment to ponder how to word her command for the best possible results.

"Invisible Servant, unbuckle and remove these straps that bind me..."

Patiently Divana waited. Within a few moments, she watched as the buckle to the first strap which held her arms and torso was slowly unclasped and tossed aside, as though unseen hands were at work. She considered herself fortunate that Veros had underestimated her, relief embracing her as the second strap was removed as well, the two which held her legs following soon after in descending order.

Wasting no time, Divana sprung up from the slab.

I hope it's not too late to help the others..

Quickly reclaiming her torch and pack, she grabbed the Wand of Magic Negation and tucked it into her belt. Scooping up the diamond skull that she knew to contain Veros' life force, she rushed from the ghastly chamber in hopes that she had in her possession the means to defeat the dark sorcerer once and for all.

"It's a good thing you still had the Invisible Servant hanging around." Peter said.

Jennifer nodded her head in agreement.

"Yeah, although I would have never thought to use it if it weren't for Amy."

Amy only grinned in reply.

Turning his attention to his sister, Kevin continued with the game. "After escaping Veros' lab, you find yourself back in the main corridor. From further down the tunnel, you can hear the sounds of battle."

"That would be us..." Jake chimed in with a grin.

"Do I see Veros?" Josh asked.

Kevin nodded. "He's emerging from the rubble a few yards away."

"I'm gonna run on down there and see if I can help." Jennifer declared. "I'll command the Invisible servant to stay with me and carry the torch to light the hall for me."

"Hey, good idea." Amy grinned.

"Alright, you hurry on down the tunnel." Kevin replied to his sister before turning to Josh. "In the meantime..."

The sounds of the battle continued to fill the chamber as Halvar's gaze remained on Veros. The lich held his side with a rotting hand as he limped forward, a clear sign that the blow from Halvar's weapon had injured the creature.

Powers of Light, protect me...

Halvar leveled the hammer as Veros stood.

"You fool..." he hissed. "Even with such a weapon you cannot destroy me."

Halvar frowned.

"We shall see."

Veros held out his hand, closing it before him as though he had taken a hold of something. A slender staff of blackened wood suddenly flickered into view, seeming to materialize out of thin air to be in his grasp. Reaching a length to nearly match that of Veros' height, the staff's top widened into a bulbous mass that twisted and gnarled to form depictions of agonized, screaming visages. Halvar readied his shield, not knowing what power the weapon possessed as his foe strode forward.

The end of the staff struck hard against the shield as Veros lunged forward, the sheer force sending Halvar several steps back. Pulling the staff back, Veros repositioned it for a forehand swing. Halvar quickly ducked as the stick cut through the air above his head. Rising, Halvar was again staggered, spun around as his shield was struck by backhand blow from the staff. Turning, he thrust the end of the hammer forward.

"Powers of Light, push back the darkness!"

A sudden burst of brilliant white light exploded from the hammer. Shielding his rotting visage with his free hand, Veros hissed while gliding backward; seeming to levitate from the ground in his retreat. Readying the hammer to strike again, Halvar charged.

Veros pointed the staff, a shimmering plane of force materializing before him in the likeness of a large kite shield.

Halvar frowned.

A Mystic Shield Spell...

Undaunted, he closed in fast, his face contorting in rage as blow after blow from the war hammer rained down against the lich's mystical protection.

Several yards away, Alaina Grimm and Darrius struggled on. Without the power of The Rod to replenish his undead legions, the trio had finally managed to turn the tide, Alaina managing to reach the inert relic with little opposition from the zombies as Grimm and Darrius dealt with their quickly dwindling numbers.

"Hurry up and destroy the blasted thing!" Grimm yelled as he and Darrius each sliced off two more heads, thus finally vanquishing the last of Veros' undead minions. As Alaina lifted her sword to bring it down on The Rod, she caught sight of Halvar's continuing battle with Veros. Frozen in shock, she watched as Veros dropped the Mystic Shield to suddenly thrust the staff forward. Caught mid attack, Halvar was struck in the chest; crashing onto his back as he was sent to slide several feet away. He slowly rolled over onto his forearms, the wind knocked out of him as he desperately struggled to stand once more.

"No." Alaina gasped.

Sensing victory, Veros slowly stalked toward Halvar. "You battle against forces beyond your ken cleric," he rasped. "Now you die."

Abandoning her task of destroying The Rod, Alaina turned and dashed to Halvar's aid, with Grimm and Darrius rushing to assist upon seeing her flight. Looking up from Halvar, Veros' mouth shaped into a putrid grin at the sight of the charging trio. "Cretins..." he whispered while pointing the staff.

The screams of a thousand tortured souls shook the chamber walls. Blasted by the sheer force that erupted from the staff, Alaina, Grimm, and Darrius all slid across the floor as they were knocked back. Returning the staff to rest upended, Veros addressed Halvar once more.

"You shall be the first to die."

Veros raised his free hand above his head. Electrical arcs began to crackle and coalesce around his open hand's fingers as he chanted menacingly.

"Mordoro Rokbarros."

Without warning, Divana charged through the entrance to the chamber. Rushing past her other prone allies, she leaped in front of Halvar. Still clutching the diamond skull which contained Veros' life force under one arm, she quickly produced the Wand of Magic Negation with the other.

"Nakurra Kabarross!" the lich hissed as he flung his arm out toward his target.

"Lakkarr Ordellios!" Divana cried out while pointing the wand.

A thunderous explosion again shook the chamber walls as a bolt of lightning shot forth from Veros' outstretched fingers. The wand glowed brilliantly in Divana's hand as Veros' attack suddenly erupted in a harmless pyrotechnic display.

"You..." Veros glared before suddenly rushing forward.

Divana gasped as the lich was again upon her before she could react. The end of the lich's staff found its mark as it was thrust into chest, her face twisting in pain as she was sent flailing. The diamond skull dropped from her grasp, landing on the floor next to Halvar as her wand flew off to land several feet away. Crashing hard onto her back, Divana held her chest, the pain from the blow forcing her into a near fetal position.

Twisting around, Halvar swung the war hammer up and outward, managing to catch Veros in the jaw. The blow was merely glancing in nature, yet still enough to send the lich reeling as he spun and staggered.

Slowly, Veros turned to glare at Halvar over his shoulder. The red pinpoints of light in his empty eye sockets remained on the target of his ire as he gripped a dislocated jaw within one decaying hand. The unmistakable cracking of bone followed as he angrily yanked the jaw to one side while pushing it upward. Working it several times to make sure it was popped back into place correctly, he rose again to his full height as he turned to face Halvar.

Still resting upon his hands and knees, Halvar turned to the skull of pure diamond that lay on the floor at his side, a wave of realization suddenly washing over him.

By the Powers! Veros' phylactery! Surely this is it!

Halvar tossed a glance of caution toward Vero's, a loud roar bursting from Veros as the lich charged. With little time, Halvar again turned his attention to Veros' phylactery.

"Powers of Light, grant me thy might!"

White flame engulfed the war hammer as Halvar raised it above his head. Magic had wrought the skull that contained Veros' life force. He hoped and prayed that the divine power being channeled through him would destroy it as he brought the hammer down with all of the strength that he could muster. The stone floor beneath the skull cracked from the impact. Veros' phylactery had remained intact.

No...

A hand suddenly seized Halvar by the throat as Veros was upon him. His hammer dropped to the floor with a heavy clang as he gripped at the wrist of Veros' outstretched arm. He winced as the lich squeezed.

"I am going to crush the life right out of you." Veros rasped.

Out of his eye's corner, Halvar suddenly noticed a soft yellowish glow emanating from the floor, a sense of hope flooding him as he again glanced at the phylactery. A series of large cracks had formed along the skull's top where he had struck it, light pouring through them as they slowly started to lengthen. In a sudden burst of radiance, the phylactery broke apart.

Veros' jaw dropped as he released a sudden heave. Dropping his staff, he clutched at his neck in a manner similar to one having trouble getting his breath. A low groan started deep within him, its volume soon rising to a full-fledged scream. Still held by the throat, Halvar watched as Veros crumbled to dust right before his eyes. Massaging his throat,

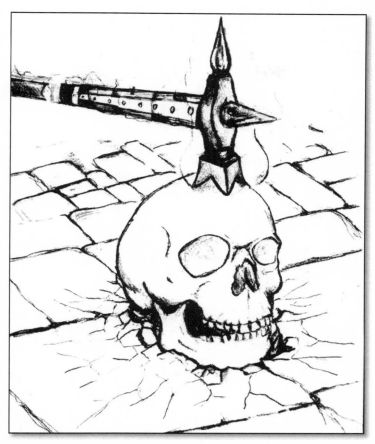

he slowly stood and looked back to the others. Alaina, Grimm, Darrius, and Divana all struggled to their feet.

All soon gathered around The Rod of Veros, still lying in the spot where it had fell. A bout of silence passed as Grimm gave a nod of his head to Halvar.

"Finish this." Alaina urged.

Raising the hammer one more time, he brought it down on The Rod. The chunk of obsidian at its end exploded, the femur shaped length of ivory soon after crumbling to dust.

The group turned at the sudden sound of grinding stone. All spotted the throne at the apex of the stairway at the chamber's back, the seat of bones sliding up the wall to reveal a previously hidden doorway. Tossing glances to one another, the group readied their weapons and began climbing the stone steps. Reaching the top they cautiously peeked through the open portal.

Two lit sconces along the back wall of the chamber revealed a large book shelf that rested against the wall to the group's left, books and scroll cases neatly lined up and stacked along its shelves. Two sturdy looking wooden chests sat open at the wall to the right, their tops overflowing with copper, silver, and gold coins as a crystal sphere rested on a stone pedestal in the room's center. All in the group exchanged grins and relieved sighs, a deep laugh bursting from Grimm as the group prepared to collect the spoils of their hard fought victory.

CHAPTER
10
The Heroes Return

Y es!" Jake cried while extending his arms and eyes upward. All at the gaming table looked on as he suddenly broke into a seated dance routine. While swaying from side to side, his fists touched together at the thumbs as his arms shot in and out in a wide circular motion, each movement the direction opposite of that which his body rocked. Amy and Jennifer only shook their heads in disbelief as Peter arched an eyebrow at Jake's antics.

"Really, dude?"

"Ok, how much XP and treasure do we get?" Jake said, abruptly ending his victory dance.

"You each get eight grand for defeating Veros and the zombies," Kevin stated. "In the treasure room, there is a total of five thousand gold, silver, and copper coins, respectively, as well as all of the books and scrolls that are on the shelves."

"Are any of them magical?" Jennifer asked.

"Most of them are on ancient history, alchemy, and other things like that," Kevin replied. "Five of them look to you like they may be spell books, though, and all of the scrolls look like they may have spells on them that you have never seen before."

"That's all yours, along with his crystal ball," Amy said to Jennifer.

"Just remember, Agamemnon frowns on the use of necromancy," Kevin warned.

"That's ok," Jennifer replied. "I don't wanna make zombies. They're gross."

"We'll gather up those bags of gold, silver, and copper and split it into even shares later," Josh said while turning to Kevin. "I'll use my healing spells on everyone before we leave."

"Fair enough." Kevin nodded. "You gather up the treasure and start the journey home."

"Agamemnon and the others were preparing for an assault on the cities," Amy recollected. "Maybe we should head to the capital. Hopefully we'll meet up with Agamemnon and the others there."

"The trip back is more or less uneventful," Kevin continued. "You make it back to Grafton with little difficulty in pretty much the same amount of time that it took you to make it to Veros' tower. In Grafton, you pick up your mounts again, and from there you ride west for another day, following the road to pass through Illingrad again and all the way to Adrinia..."

The mountain peaks had begun to touch the sun's base in the early stages of its descent. Stopping their mounts at the base of a hill, the group stared up at a large keep which stood at its apex. Banners of bright red that bore the likeness of a golden dragon on them waved proudly in the wind above its gray stone walls.

"Looks like Adrinia held out," Darrius observed as the keep's walls remained intact, showing only minimal damage as a result of the undead siege that all knew had transpired here in their absence.

"Let's go." Alaina smiled. The mounts that she and the others rode were still loaded down with the treasure from Veros' crypt as they continued up the road leading to the large wooden gates of the marvelous structure.

Slowly swinging inward, the gates opened as the group approached, revealing white buildings with red-tiled roofs. Loud cheers and upraised hands greeted them as they rode amid the masses of elf, dwarf, and man that had gathered within Adrinia's walls.

"Nothing quite like a hero's homecoming, huh, Grimm?" Darrius said. The dwarf gave only a grunt and a nod of his head in reply as a grin peeked out from beneath his thick red beard.

Stopping their mounts, everyone in the group saw Agamemnon moving through the ocean of people with gnarled staff in hand. An elf and dwarf walked at his side, each producing a smile as the group dismounted to join them.

"Agamemnon!" Divana cried out in excitement as she rushed toward her aged mentor, wrapping both arms around the wizard in a joyous hug.

"Well done, child," Agamemnon said with a chuckle, returning the embrace with a single arm of his own as Grimm and Darrius stopped before their fathers. Ulfgar Ironforge and Ahiramil Goldleaf each placed a congratulatory hand upon the shoulders of their respective sons.

As Alaina and Halvar looked on, the crowds parted for a middle-aged man who approached. Finely-made red robes with gold trim hid his frame, and a trio of men in silvery full plate armor flanked him on both sides. Strands of long, straight brown hair draped over the man's shoulders from beneath a golden crown that sat upon his head.

"By the Powers of Light!" Halvar exclaimed.

"That's King Aldrich!" Alaina added.

The king and his entourage of armored knights stopped before Halvar and Alaina, who lowered themselves to kneel. "Please rise, my friends," King Aldrich said.

Alaina and Halvar stood once more, joined soon after by Grimm, Darrius, Divana, and the others who had gathered with them in celebration. A broad smile formed beneath King Aldrich's thick brown mustache. "We owe you brave heroes a great debt of gratitude," he said. "You have made these lands safe once more from the forces of evil."

All looked on as the king turned to one of his knights, taking from him a piece of rolled-up parchment. "Please accept this as a token of my appreciation," he said, offering his reward.

Taking the parchment in hand, Alaina unrolled it, holding it open with a hand at its top and bottom as Halvar, Grimm, Darrius, and Divana gathered around her to see. "Do my eyes deceive me?" Grimm asked excitedly. "Or is that a treasure map?!"

A depiction of the Adrinian kingdom was spread out upon the parchment's surface, a large X in bold red marking the center of the Brom Mountains in the kingdom's northern region.

"Looks like more adventures await you, brave heroes." Agamemnon chuckled.

The five could only stare at the map, each quietly pondering what dangers and riches could possibly await those who would be brave enough to make the journey.

With soft eyes, Agamemnon watched the five heroes in silent musing. A warm grin slowly formed beneath his beard at his thoughts.

Oh, yes... more adventures, indeed...

EPILOGUE

Happily Ever After

Holy crap, it's five in the morning," Jake observed while looking at his wrist watch.

"Wow!" Jennifer exclaimed. "We played the whole night!"

"That's pretty easy to do with this game," Amy said. "It's pretty much what we usually do."

"Well, that's the end of the adventure," Kevin said. "I'll award you guys another one thousand experience points for completing the quest and for good roleplaying."

Jennifer turned to her brother. "I had a lot of fun. I wanna play again sometime."

Kevin grinned as everyone began packing up their gaming books. "Well, we won't be able to play next weekend. We're going with Mom and Dad to Florida for two weeks' vacation, remember?"

"Yeah," Jennifer replied. "You could bring the books and the dice, though. I wanna play some more. I like Divana."

"I suppose I could bring the game." Kevin smirked.

"Well, I think I'm gonna head home and go to bed," Peter said.

"Same here," Jake added with a stretch and a yawn. "I bet I pass out soon as my head hits the pillow."

"We'll probably play again when we get back from vacation," Kevin said. "I'll keep everyone's character sheet until next time."

"Halvar will hold onto the treasure map until we can all get together again," Josh declared, writing it down under the list of equipment on his character sheet before handing it to Kevin along with the other players.

"Hand us all those dirty dishes," Peter said as he shouldered his backpack. "We can put 'em all in the dishwasher on our way out."

"Thanks, guys," Kevin replied as everyone did their part to collect the plates and glasses that were on the table. "I'll come down later and pick up all these cans," he added, gesturing around the table and floor to the aluminum soda cans that were scattered about the seating area.

After you get up around four in the afternoon, right?" Josh added playfully.

"Pretty much, yeah," Kevin replied with a smirk and tired eyes.

Making their way back upstairs, Kevin and Jennifer saw everyone to the kitchen door once the dirty dishes were all placed in the dishwasher. "See you guys in school," Kevin said, with Amy, Josh, Jake, and Peter all giving a farewell after their departure. Closing and locking the kitchen door behind his friends, Kevin turned to his sister. "You really wanna play while we're on vacation, huh?" he said.

Jennifer smiled. "Yeah, I do."

"Alright, I'll bring the books," Kevin replied with a grin as he and Jennifer headed off to their separate rooms to finally go to sleep.

Outside, the sun had begun peeking over the hills as the four friends climbed onto their bikes.

"See you guy's at school Monday," Peter said.

"See you later," Josh replied as Jake and Peter rode off to their respective homes.

As Josh watched the two for a few moments, he suddenly noticed that Amy sat upon her own bike, parked at his side as her lips shaped into a warm smile.

"So what are you doing next weekend?"

"Well..." Josh stammered. "I'm... I'm not really sure."

He felt his cheeks flush as Amy's smile remained. "You know..." she started. "The way you kept coming to my rescue in the game, I think that was kinda sweet."

Josh stood silent, unsure of how to respond. He wished he had the confidence that he had portrayed all through the night as Halvar Lightbringer.

"If you aren't doing anything next Saturday, why don't you come over?" Amy asked, the question sounding more like a suggestion. "We can play some video games, maybe watch a movie or something."

"Uhhh...sure..." Josh finally stammered after a few seconds. Amy's eyes were soft as she suddenly leaned toward him. His eyes nearly bugged out of his head as her lips gently touched his cheek.

"I like you." Amy grinned. "You're really sweet."

Josh could only smile sheepishly.

"So you'll come over next Saturday?" she asked again, sounding hopeful.

Josh nodded, a sigh of elation escaping him, as he'd never seen a girl take an interest in him before. "Yeah. Sure. I'll be there."

"Great!" Amy beamed. "I'll see you in school 'til then."

With that, Amy rode off down the street.

Josh watched her for a few moments as her bike began carrying her into the distance.

What are you doing?! Go after her!

"Hey, Amy! Wait up!" he suddenly yelled, quickly peddling in an effort to catch up to her as he finally managed to shake off his shyness, if for only a brief moment.

Amy slowed down, allowing Josh to ride up to her side.

"You... you mind if I ride with you?" he asked, stammering again. "My house is on the way..."

Amy giggled, finding his shyness cute. "No, not at all. I'd like that."

Josh smiled as he and Amy continued down the street together, suddenly finding the real world to be a more magical place than he had ever imagined.

About Author

Trace Richards often resides in the wilds between the small Missouri towns of Clarksville and Louisiana, while at other times he takes up residence within Louisiana city limits. As a longtime gamer, he would like to credit Gary Gygax as one of the inspirations for this book and for many summers of dice rolling. He is also a practitioner of the martial arts.

Trace will continue his ambitions in the ways of both the pen and the sword as he works on future stories.